QUICK AND THE DEAD

QUICKSILVER: BOOK THREE

JOSIE JAFFREY

CONTENT WARNINGS & SERIES RECAPS

There is a full list of content warnings at the back of this book, and also available at Josie's website at the link on the left below.

Recaps of the Silverse books are available on Josie's website at the link on the right below.

CONTENT WARNINGS

www.josiejaffrey.com/content-warnings

SERIES RECAPS

www.josiejaffrey.com/series-recaps

By Josie Jaffrey

Stories from the Silverse: the World of the Silver

The Seekers Series
Killian's Dead (short story prequel, free to Josie's
subscribers)
May Day
Judgement Day
Winta's Day
Valentine's Day
Dark Days
End of Days

The QuickSilver Trilogy
Kill Me Quick
A Quick Study
Quick and the Dead
QuickSilver Omnibus Edition

The Solis Invicti Series
A Bargain in Silver
The Price of Silver
Bound in Silver
The Silver Bullet

The Sovereign Trilogy
The Gilded King
The Silver Queen
The Blood Prince

Silverse Serialised Stories
Dead Box
Dead Road

Silverse Short Stories
Encounters: Silverse Short Stories

1

IN THE COLD stillness of the wine cellar beneath his mansion, Bartholomew Sometimes-Roberts stood looking at seven zombies that wouldn't die.

God knew he'd tried to help them along, as the three broken figures on the floor amply demonstrated. He'd dismembered, decapitated and disembowelled, but all he'd got for his troubles was a slightly shorter pile of zombie pieces, moving in that eerily hypnotic way of theirs, like waves across the sea, synchronous and undulating. They flinched away from him as he chained the ones that hadn't been reduced to puddles back up against the cellar wall, as though they recognised the threat he presented to them. They shouldn't be clever enough to react with fear, even after he'd cut a couple of them down, but they'd been flinching from the moment he'd walked into the room.

That wasn't just abnormal, it was fascinating.

There had always been the zombies. They went hand in hand with the Silver, the failure that resulted whenever someone tried to turn a new Silver and got it wrong. The zombies were the remnants, the dregs that remained once the potential Silver evaporated, or at least that was how

Bartholomew had always thought of them.

Waste products.

But these new creatures that Bella had somehow created with Dr Ross's serum? He wasn't sure what they were.

Across the cellar, someone moaned.

'Oh, good,' said Bartholomew. 'You're awake.'

Bayly looked at Bartholomew, then at his lover Enzo lying unconscious beside him, then at the zombies, and finally at the chains around his wrists.

'You drained me?' he asked.

'Didn't have to,' said Bartholomew. 'Your old friend Digs did that for you.'

Bayly raised an eyebrow stoically. 'Kulika told you about that?'

Bartholomew tutted, then surveyed Bayly disapprovingly. He leaned back against the stone plinth in the centre of the room. 'She didn't need to say a thing. What am I always telling you, Bayly? There's no point trying to hide from me. I see everything.'

Then he pushed the lid of the plinth, sending it crashing onto the brick floor. There was a moment of utter silence, followed by an exhalation that sounded like paper flapping in the wind. A black, twisted thing that might once have been a hand hooked itself over the edge of the open plinth – sarcophagus, more properly – and tightened its grip on the stone.

Bartholomew grinned. 'I thought the two of you might like some time to catch up,' he said. 'It's been so long.' Then he put his hands in his pockets and hummed to himself happily as he climbed back up the brick stairs to the kitchen, accompanied by a symphony of screams.

Several storeys above, in the suite next to Bartholomew's, Kulika Yadav was flicking restlessly through her phone.

By now – the early hours of Wednesday morning – the discovery of Cara Alton's body was all over the news. She'd been found by a jogger, propped up against a tree in a suburban neighbourhood just fifty miles from her parents' house in Oklahoma. And how she'd been positioned…

If the jogger hadn't taken photos before the police arrived and sold them to some disreputable online "journalists", the world would never have known how she'd been positioned, but he was a scumbag, so he'd done both of those things.

Kulika had a suspicion that Bartholomew was somehow responsible for the scumbag. He'd always had a talent for bringing out people's baser impulses. But whether it was his fault or not, the whole world now knew that Cara Alton had been sitting with her legs crossed, shirtless to display the silver handprint on her stomach, with her short skirt bunched up around her hips to display the bite mark on her femoral artery. There had been no blood in her body, which had been so cold that when the jogger touched her – because of course the little pervert touched her – he'd left some of his own skin behind on hers.

Served him right.

But Kulika was worried.

The rumours were churning more quickly now than they had when Cara first disappeared: it was aliens in the beginning, then it was special effects, but already the media was starting to report the girl's death as a vampiric mystery. It was as though they *wanted* to believe there was something paranormal going on. At this rate, by the time the autopsy was finished no one would be able to deny it, and with the current level of public outcry, no one would be able to cover it up either. Then the stage would be set for Bartholomew's grand revelation. He had been right: it was a good plan.

Kulika wished like hell that she didn't have to be part of

it, but she'd made a deal with the devil to keep the woman she loved safe. Soon, it would be time for her to pay up.

In the room next to Kulika's, Evita Khalyed woke before dawn to find her best friend kneeling at her bedside with her head pillowed on Evita's hand. She was fast asleep.

That was a shame. Evita didn't want to involve Quick in what she had to do next, and Quick had always been a light sleeper. Now that she was one of the Silver, with all the enhanced senses that came along with it, Evita had no doubt that Quick would wake up the moment she tried to move.

Bugger.

Then she noticed Xiaoyu, lately of the blood cellar, occupying the room's other bed. The human was on a drip, which was enough to give Evita pause. Since when did Bartholomew give enough of a shit about any of the humans on his property to bother nursing one back to health?

Strange indeed.

But there'd be time for questions later. First, Evita needed to get out of this bed, track down Bartholomew fucking Roberts, and nail him to the wall. Through the heart, for preference.

The crew would kill her, of course. She wasn't naïve enough to think that she could get away with murdering their captain without repercussions, if she managed to do it at all. That's why she needed to give Quick the slip first, so she could do it alone. Then she could free them both, even if she had to die to do it.

Later, though, when the time was right. If the past few weeks she'd spent trapped in a coffin with a blood-starved pirate had taught her nothing else, Evita Khalyed had at least proved one thing to herself: she was good at waiting.

On a property abutting the Cooper River, the Charleston

Historical Society was preparing to unveil its greatest accomplishment to date. Funded generously by an anonymous private donor, and requiring an army of rare and specialised craftsmen to build, the replica of the fourth-rate frigate the *Royal Fortune* was truly a sight to behold.

Aloysius Truman, Society Chairman, was obsessed with it. He'd spent his long, dull life dreaming of pirate ships, and now he had one right in front of him. And not just any old pirate ship, but the flagship of the most successful pirate captain of all time, Bartholomew Roberts. The ship on which he'd *died*, no less. As Aloysius stood in the shipbuilding hangar, watching the painters stroke the last letters onto the prow of the incredible vessel, he could almost hear the clash of blades, smell the gunpowder, feel the sea spray on his bare forearms. Lord, what a rush.

He could almost see *her* too, the woman who haunted his dreams.

The original *Royal Fortune* had started out its life as a British Royal Navy frigate called *Onslow*, before being captured and repurposed by Roberts as his flagship. There had been women on board that ship, Aloysius knew. Those women had become captives of the crew, and they had been mistreated in ways that even the court transcripts had balked at reporting. Most were released. One, a blonde-haired waif, had disappeared without a trace. That disappearance had preoccupied Aloysius all his life, both mightily and thrillingly. Perhaps she'd dressed up as a man and joined the crew, or perhaps – more enticingly – Roberts had fallen in love with her and decided to break his own code to keep her close to him as he pirated his way from one side of the Atlantic to the other.

Perhaps.

Driven by every tantalising mention he'd uncovered in his

amateur investigations – a blonde woman reported seizing a ship off the Ivory Coast, a fleeting reference in Captain Johnson's famous compendium of pirates, an eighteenth-century artist's sketch of a windswept woman on a ship's prow annotated with the letters "KUL" – Aloysius had diverted the society's attention increasingly towards the woman known to history only as *Kulika*.

That had become a source of resentment amongst the society's membership. It was bad enough that Aloysius had become chairman without proper academic credentials, but now they had to suffer his fanciful ideas as well? But they didn't have much choice. Suffice it to say that Aloysius's money was as old as the central Charleston Rainbow Row house in which he lived, and running the society was a surprisingly costly enterprise.

But really. Crossdressing women? Love affairs on the high seas? These were the artefacts of tacky films and bad novels. If Aloysius's money hadn't been keeping the society afloat for the past decade, that kind of bull crap would never have been tolerated.

Then he'd brought them this commission, and suddenly the society members had been willing to tolerate a lot more. They'd happily let Aloysius reconstruct an elaborate ladies' boudoir in the cabin next to the captain's to sate his fantasy, because it allowed each of them free rein for their own particular specialisms, and there were a lot of those amongst the society. Several years and several fortunes later, all forty cannon were now in working order. The glass for the windows at the stern of the ship – glazing the captain's cabin, state room and ward room – had all been hand blown in local workshops using traditional methods appropriate for the period. The history department head at the local university had gone wild with period furnishings and armaments, at astronomical expense. The donor hadn't batted an eyelid as the costs soared. In fact, he'd let all of them put their own stamp on the project, making just one stipulation of his own: the ship was to be called the *Primus's Fortune*.

Aloysius fully intended to use it to make his.

2

'GREETINGS!' BARTHOLOMEW CALLED into the pre-dawn air, addressing the hundreds of Silver who were gathered on the riverbanks at the edge of his property. 'And welcome to the Golden Age of my Primacy!'

The younger ones didn't get the reference to the Golden Age of piracy, but Kulika and the other Silver did. She wondered then if the reason Bartholomew had dragged them all down here in the dark had less to do with the dramatic silhouette he would shortly cast against the sunrise, and more to do with their proximity to the water. When the frigate rounded the turn in the river, sailing on the morning breeze, her suspicion was confirmed.

'What the…'

'Impressive, right?' said the man beside her, an older Silver Kulika didn't recognise. 'I helped draw up the plans. Replica of the *Royal Fortune*. I used to be a shipwright, you know,' he added with some pride.

'Hey, don't you know who that is?' the man next to the shipwright said to him, speaking in a horrified, hushed whisper as he shepherded his friend away.

Kulika didn't stop them. She was still picking her jaw up

off the floor. Good thing the river here was both wide and deep, because otherwise the frigate wouldn't have fit down the channel. It was enormous, but simultaneously smaller than Kulika remembered it being.

The sight of it made her sick.

'We're not all going to fit on that,' someone muttered from behind Kulika.

'That's not the point, dumbass,' someone else replied. 'We're not supposed to. It's a symbol. Don't you get it?'

A symbol. Well, they were right about that.

The Onslow.

The Royal Fortune.

Same ship, same shit: bloodshed, fire, death.

Of course the vessel sailing their way was a replica, because Kulika would have been able to smell the real ship from miles away. Its decks had been swabbed with gore, its hold filled with coffins full of treasure. It had been a ghost ship, inhabited by the living dead.

Bartholomew wanted to relive those glory days. Kulika just wanted to burn them from her memory, and from the memory of the world.

'I've gathered you all here for a momentous occasion,' Bartholomew continued, as the dawn breeze picked up long locks of his glossy brown hair and played with them. 'Today, not only are we celebrating the launch of the *Primus's Fortune*, but also the launch of the reign of the Silver!'

Cheers erupted from the riverbanks with an enthusiasm that Kulika couldn't share.

'We used to be gods on this earth,' Bartholomew continued, gesturing widely at the crowd. From the way they nodded along, it was clear these were words they'd heard before. 'We used to *rule*. But what are we now? Rats and cockroaches, forced into the shadows where they can't find us, feeding on scraps. Well, not anymore. By this evening, the details of Cara Alton's autopsy will hit the news, and tonight we are hosting the biggest party this mansion has ever seen. There will be journalists here to cover the unveiling of the *Primus's Fortune*, with live feeds around the world. Then we'll show them what we really are, and exactly how low they should bow.'

The ship came in to dock behind Bartholomew just as the dawn broke over the horizon, bathing him in an eerie red glow.

'Tonight, my crew,' he said, 'there will be blood.'

Apparently dawn wasn't too early – or too late – for a party at the mansion. The part of the crew that had sailed the ship downriver had all eagerly disembarked, heading for the pool. Someone was behind the bar before the cheering that followed Bartholomew's speech had even died down, and the crew were all either carrying on drinking from the night before or getting an early start on the day. It didn't seem to matter one way or another; everyone was joining in.

Everyone except Kulika, that was. She'd left the kids to it and taken a single bottle of beer down to the dock, where she could dangle her feet off the end and fish for gators. It was a beautiful morning, which made Kulika feel worse somehow. The sun glinted off the river in sheets of blinding light, its warmth soaked into the marshland, and the whole place smelled of green things breathing heavily in preparation for the heat the day would bring.

She had come here to be alone, but she didn't stay that way for long. She was only halfway down her beer when a confident tread on the creaking wood of the dock behind her heralded Bartholomew's approach.

'What do you think of her, then?' Bartholomew said, gesturing at the ship that loomed over them both. 'Beautiful, isn't she?'

'She's a bad memory,' Kulika muttered.

'Oh, don't be like that.' He sat down next to her, pulling off his shoes so he could dangle his own feet in the water. 'She's a marvel. Some of the craftsmen had to relearn techniques from scratch. She's a feat of un-modern engineering.'

'She's too big for the dock. Too big for the river.'

'Then it's a good thing I'm not planning to keep her here long.' He leaned back on his hands, tilted his face to the sun, then gave Kulika an assessing look. 'You don't like her.'

'I just don't see the point of her,' Kulika argued. 'It's the twenty-first century, not the eighteenth. Why would anyone need a sailing frigate?'

'To make a promise,' Bartholomew said. He looked up at the shining new wood, smiling gently to himself.

Kulika couldn't remember the last time she'd seen Bartholomew look genuinely contented. Had she ever? But here he was, beaming at an inanimate bunch of wood and sails in the same way a parent might beam at their child.

'What kind of promise?' she asked him.

'Hmm?' When he turned to her, the vague smile was still warming his face.

'What promise?' she said.

'To the crew, of better things to come. You're not the only one who misses our pirating days.'

'I don't miss them at all.'

Bartholomew scoffed emphatically; they both knew that was a lie. Kulika might be resisting it as hard as she could, but she felt the pull of the sea just as strongly as she ever had. More, even, now that she was losing Quick. She wanted to leave the land behind her and run away to the waves. She wanted to be free again, but she knew the cost of that freedom too intimately to admit the depth of her desire.

Kulika could see the future in that moment, and she hated it as much as she yearned for it. Bartholomew would play on her ambivalence, as he always had, and before long she'd be up to her elbows in blood and treasure once more. That's what the *Primus's Fortune* represented to her: total relapse.

'None of the old crew are here anyway,' Kulika pointed out. 'Except Bayly, wherever Monty's put him.'

'Somewhere safe.'

'That's what he said,' Kulika replied sceptically.

'And the others are coming tonight, for the launch. You'll see your old crew again.'

'Most of them were human,' Kulika pointed out. 'They're all dead.'

'But not Wolfrie. Not Phinchas.'

Kulika's mouth dropped open. Hearing the familiar names in Bartholomew's voice made her ache with nostalgia.

'They're coming?' she whispered.

'They are.'

Kulika eyes were filling with tears. God, why was she welling up? She hadn't cried when she'd signed over her life to Bartholomew in return for Quick's. She wasn't crying about Quick now, even though she was about to say goodbye forever and her heart was breaking. It made no sense that she should respond to the news of Wolfrie and Phinchas's return with such emotion, but it had been so long. Maybe this was just the final drop of water that had overflowed the vessel where she held her pain.

She tried to hide her reaction from Bartholomew, knowing he'd use it against her – but what motivation would he have for that now? Why bother threatening her when she had already given herself entirely into his power? On the other hand, if he wanted nothing he couldn't already take from her, why would he trouble himself to offer her such a gift?

Phinchas and Wolfrie.

Besides Bayly, they were the only true friends she'd had in Bartholomew's crew, and the only reason she'd hesitated to leave. She loved them like siblings, but she'd spent the past hundred years trying to forget they'd ever existed, because of what they represented to her.

'If you're messing with me—'

'This is my promise to them,' he said, waving up at the ship. 'And they're my promise to you.'

'Of?'

'Crew. Real crew. I'm not completely unfeeling, Kulika. I know you need more than these new Silver, who look at you with more reverence and fear than kindness. They're just your army. Wolfrie and Phinchas can be your generals.'

'And Bayly?'

'Will serve his sentence. After that… we'll talk.'

There would be an after, though. That was more than Kulika had dared hope for.

Phinchas and Wolfrie.

Last she'd heard, they'd been causing havoc on the west coast in the entertainment industry. They could be sharks, those two, when they got together. It was the perfect playground for the pair of grifters, and one she hadn't thought they'd ever want to leave.

'What did you have to offer them to get them back here?' she asked.

'Not much,' he said, that contented smile returning to his face. 'Just you.'

'Me?'

'They missed you, Kulika. We all missed you. After you left… Well, I told you I would hold us together, and I will. The new crew with the covenant, and the old crew with something stronger still.'

Kulika's blood ran cold. She looked at Bartholomew, waiting for the word she knew was coming: *blood*. She waited despite knowing, because that's what Bartholomew expected, but in the end he didn't deliver that word. Instead, he tilted his head, letting his hair tumble over his shoulder as he assessed her.

'Honestly, if I didn't know better,' he said, 'I'd think you were already regretting our deal.'

'No backing out,' Kulika said sharply. 'We made a bargain.'

'I haven't forgotten.' He reached out and took her hand in his, rubbing his thumb gently over the new covenant mark that nestled in her palm. 'Have you?'

'I'll keep my side,' she promised. 'If you keep yours.'

'Well, then.'

A heron came to land on the far side of the river, then strode through the shallows in search of morsels to snap up in its beak. Until the music started up, sending it flapping off into the sky once more.

Kulika turned to look over her shoulder at the pool. Someone had dragged a tower of speakers out from the block and was using them to blast thudding beats towards the party, but not all of the crew were joining in; some of them were getting ready for tonight's press conference. Silver were carrying lights and rigs and boxes in a never-ending procession from the driveway to the riverbanks. At this stage, Kulika couldn't work out exactly what they were building, but it looked like they were preparing for a performance and a half.

Kulika found her gaze dragged back towards the house, to the window next to her own. With any luck, Quick and her friends would still be asleep behind it, despite the noise. The blinds were drawn and dark.

'I'll send the kid to give them their marching orders,' Bartholomew said, following the direction of her gaze. 'Our Patience—'

Kulika scowled at the possessive pronoun, just as she was sure Bartholomew had planned her to. Even now, with all the assurances he had, he was still trying to get a rise out of her.

And succeeding.

'Just Patience, then,' he corrected himself, with a smile. 'She and her friends will be out of here this morning. You have my word.'

'So soon?'

'You wanted to draw it out? Kulika, our deal was clear.'

'I know that.'

'The kid's arranged a car to take them to the airport. It'll be here shortly.'

Kulika looked at him in disbelief for a moment, then pulled her feet out of the water, dried them haphazardly on the cuffs of her trousers and shoved them back into her boots.

There was a tinkling noise, and she looked over to see that Bartholomew was holding a set of keys out to her. A set of very shiny keys, with a distinctive high-end sports car logo on them that matched the emblem on Bartholomew's personal vehicle.

'I suggest you absent yourself,' he said. 'I'm planning to do the same.'

'And leave the crew here on their own, unsupervised?'

'They're not children.'

'No, they're worse: they're immature, untested Silver.'

'They'll manage. You don't need to be here to watch Patience leave.'

Which was the real problem, of course. He wanted Kulika

out of the way, so there was no risk of her reneging on their agreement.

'But...' she said, grasping for closure. 'I thought if I just said goodbye, then at least—'

'She won't take it any easier,' Bartholomew said, pretending sympathy that Kulika was certain he didn't feel. 'And in case you've forgotten, you gave up your claim on her. She's leaving the mansion today, just as you wished. We have a blood bargain, Kulika. Do you expect me to honour my part of it, or...?' His eyes drifted upwards, to the window behind which Quick and her friends were sleeping.

'No,' Kulika said quickly. 'No, I'll...' She snatched the keys from his hand. 'I'll go and check on Dr Ross at the lab. She was going to work through the night on the formula.'

'Then you can send her on her way back to Oxford and say goodbye to Drake once and for all,' Bartholomew said pointedly as he got to his feet. 'I'm going to inspect my new ship, take her for a test float. I'll be back before long, and then we'll talk. We have much to talk about, you and me. Don't we?' He reached out and tugged gently at the strand of hair that was hanging over Kulika's eye, almost playfully. That was, she knew, a bad sign; the things that put Bartholomew in a playful mood were not most people's idea of fun. 'Say, midday?' he added. 'The library, I think.'

Kulika just nodded numbly. She couldn't refuse him. Not now. Not ever again.

3

IT WAS MID-morning when Quick woke to find herself drooling on her best friend's hand.

'Oh god,' she said, wiping the moisture away with the bedsheet. 'I'm sorry. Are you okay? I didn't mean to get spit on you.'

'You snored, too,' Evita said. 'Loudly. As bloody usual.'

'I'm sorry.' Then Quick blinked as the implications of that last comment sank in. 'You remember me,' she said.

'Of course I remember you, Impatience.'

Quick laughed at the familiar nickname. It had been so long. 'I mean, you got your memory back. Kulika said you'd lost it when you turned Silver, and no one knew who you really were.'

'Right,' Evita agreed, but her expression flashed into anger, just for a moment, for reasons Quick didn't understand. 'I was Jane Doe for a while, but I had time enough to remember myself while I was locked in Bayly's treasure chest.'

'His *what*?' Quick said, horrified. 'Kulika told me he'd taken you, but she didn't say anything about—'

'Forget it.' Evita laughed. 'I'm just glad to see you.'

17

'God, yes. Me too.' Quick perched on the edge of the bed and pulled Evita gently into her arms, squeezing her as tightly as she felt was safe.

'I'm not made of glass,' Evita said. 'You can hug me properly.'

Quick did.

After six months of searching and finding nothing, and after a week stuck in this hellhole of a place battling vampires and zombies and potential emotional attachments she'd rather not dwell on right now, she had Evita in her arms. It felt good, but surreal, and a little scary given that they were both *still* stuck here in this hellhole of a place with vampires and zombies and all the rest. That might have been why Quick was crying, or maybe it was the relief of finding her best friend, but Evita couldn't judge her because she was crying too, even if she was trying to hide it.

Evita had never been very good at emotions, which was saying something, coming from Quick.

'You look better,' Quick said, holding Evita at arm's length while her friend pretended to have something in both eyes simultaneously.

'Allergies,' Evita sniffed. 'Terrible pollen in this place.'

'You don't get hay fever,' Quick said dismissively. 'Are you feeling better?'

'I'm fine,' Evita said, brushing Quick's solicitous hands away. 'I'm Silver. It's her we have to worry about.' Evita nodded towards the other bed, where Xiaoyu was just beginning to rouse.

Someone had hooked her up to a drip, which must have happened in the early hours because Quick had sat up awake most of the night and no one had come in. Xiaoyu tugged the cannula impatiently out of the back of her hand and sat up in bed. That felt miraculous enough, given the state Quick had found her in when she'd rescued her from the blood cellar, but that wasn't the only thing that had changed. Xiaoyu's eyes were brighter, her skin less pallid, her face less gaunt.

'You look better,' Quick said, looking her up and down.

'Couldn't have got much worse,' Xiaoyu commented.

She swung her legs off the side of the bed and got unsteadily to her feet. Quick managed to catch her before she fell, but only with the benefit of Silver speed.

'I'm fine,' Xiaoyu said, batting her away.

'No, you're not. You fell over. When I found you last night, you were practically dead.'

'Dehydrated,' Xiaoyu said dismissively, pushing Quick away. Quick let her, but the woman was wobbling.

'You're both fine, then?' Quick said irritably, glaring at the two of them.

'Yes,' they chorused, with equal irritation.

'You can't stand up straight,' Quick said, jabbing a finger in Xiaoyu's direction as she fell back onto her bed, 'and you're crying for the first time in maybe forever,' she added, jabbing a finger at Evita. 'You are neither of you *fine*.'

There was a knock at the door, and Monty poked his head around it. Monty, of all bloody people.

'You can leave now,' he said.

Quick sighed. 'Maybe Evita and I can go back to the dorm, but Xiaoyu can't go back to the cellar. Not like this.'

'You're not understanding me,' Monty said, slowly and loudly, as though she was hard of hearing. 'I mean you can *leave*. As in, go away. All three of you. You two are released from the covenant, officially.' He pointed at Quick and Evita. 'Your car will be here in an hour, for the airport, or wherever you want to go. If I were you, I wouldn't keep it waiting, or Bartholomew might change his mind.'

'But…'

Quick had so many questions that she didn't know where to start. Why was he letting them go now, after everything? Why them? And *how*?

But most importantly: what about Kulika?

'We can't just go,' Evita pointed out. 'We signed the covenant. We're crew. If we leave, the crew will feel it. It'll hurt them. It'll hurt *us*.'

'That's what these are for,' Monty said, pulling a couple of plastic-wrapped tubes from his pocket as he approached Evita's bed: vacutainers for collecting blood. 'Come on,' he said to Evita and Quick. 'Arms.'

Evita rolled up her sleeve and let Monty sloppily extract a vial full of blood from the vein in the crook of her elbow.

'You're not very good at this, are you?' Evita said as he pulled the needle back out.

'Did you want to do it?' he challenged.

'Yes, actually. Here.' She snatched the last vacutainer from Monty and waved Quick closer. 'Roll up your sleeve,' she said, then she applied pressure around the top of Quick's arm and gently slid the vacutainer's needle into Quick's vein.

'You've done this before,' Quick said, with a hint of accusation in her tone.

'A lot happened in the past six months,' Evita murmured. She expertly extracted the needle and sealed the vial, then passed it to Monty, saying, 'What now?'

'Now we'll do the same ritual we do when people die. The crew will forget you soon enough.'

'But what about us?' Evita asked. 'We'll still hurt for the crew, won't we? And we've got these stupid tattoos,' he said, showing him the black spot in the centre of her palm. 'How do we break the covenant without hurting ourselves?'

'Look, do you want to leave or not?' Monty said impatiently.

'Yes,' said Xiaoyu from the other bed. 'Definitely yes.'

'Well, then. Cut out the tattoos, if you want. The pain's your problem.'

Then he left, at speed, before Quick had screwed up the courage to ask about Kulika.

'Dick,' Evita commented.

But Xiaoyu was laughing. 'See?' she said. 'Ladies, it's our lucky day.'

Quick wasn't so sure, and from the look on Evita's face, it was obvious she had her own misgivings.

'I'm going to get cleaned up,' Xiaoyu said to the others, looking down at her filthy clothes. She was still wearing the dirty jeans and ripped top she'd had on when Quick had carried her out of the cellar the night before, and her skin was streaked with blood. Evita didn't look much better, though she was at least wearing clean grey sweats that covered up the worst of the grime.

'Like the kid said,' said Xiaoyu, 'let's get out of here before Bartholomew changes his mind.'

'I should wash too,' Evita said as the ensuite door closed behind Xiaoyu. 'Are we cutting these out, or…' Evita spread her fingers to show her covenant stamp.

Quick ran her fingers over her own, feeling the way the skin had healed right over it, without any texture at all, as though it had always been there. The skin would heal just as cleanly if they cut them out, she supposed, but she hadn't forgotten the pain from the initial stamping. It was going to hurt like a bastard.

Still, she really, desperately wanted it gone.

'I'll do yours, you do mine?' Evita suggested.

'What are best friends for?' Quick said darkly.

Quick tried to get through the whole thing without thinking, because if she thought too hard about it, she was going to chicken out. She fetched a knife from the kitchen, and alcohol for antiseptic. They went as fast as they could, cutting shallow and sure, but by the time they were done, the sheets of Evita's bed looked like a crime scene, even if the wounds had already healed beneath the blood.

Quick had been right. It had hurt like a bastard.

But she was *free*. They were both free.

'There's another bathroom along the corridor,' Evita said shakily. 'Do you mind if I…?'

Quick kept forgetting that Evita had lived in this place for months before she'd been been taken captive by Bayly. She knew the mansion much better than Quick did, and had clearly held a much higher rank than Quick had managed in her short tenure here if she'd been up on this floor before. Other than her brief visits with Kulika, Quick had never made it above the ground floor, and she'd certainly never had permission to explore.

'You go ahead,' Quick said, then she watched as Evita extracted herself from the bedsheets, alert to any sign that she might need help. She moved easily, and she looked strong, but she couldn't hide the dried blood covering her bare feet.

'Vee,' Quick said, with shock.

Evita followed her gaze to her gore-painted toes.

'It's fine,' Evita said dismissively. 'I'm healed. Anyway, don't you have stuff to fetch from the dorms? Goodbyes to say?'

Quick felt like her best friend was trying to get rid of her. After so many months apart, that stung a little, but with everything Evita had been through, she knew she had to tread carefully. Evita tended to get spikier when she was hurt, not softer. That wasn't uncommon for kids with their kinds of histories; your protective instincts kicked in and you coiled in on yourself, lashing out to push people away rather than opening up to pull them close. It was only natural, Quick knew, but still.

Six months.

'We've only got an hour,' Evita added pointedly. 'Less, now.'

'One goodbye, maybe,' Quick admitted, thinking longingly of Kulika's sea grey eyes.

'Then I'd go now. This might be your only chance.'

With that, Evita shoved her bloody toes into a pair of socks that had been left on the floor by the bed and padded out into the corridor, with every appearance of health.

Left alone in the room, Quick felt strangely deflated. She'd come here looking for Evita, and she'd found her. Not only that, but she'd found Xiaoyu as well. Now they were all leaving together – changed, certainly, but safe. That was a triumph in the circumstances.

So why did Quick feel so empty?

If she'd been a better person, the answer would have had something to do with all the humans who were still stuck down in the blood cellar, but that wasn't it. The real answer was this: the idea of leaving Kulika behind made her ache.

Quick returned to the dorms to clear out her bunk, passing all the other Silver in the middle of a colossal pool party. There was an electricity in the air that made Quick glad they were leaving now, a sense of anticipation that sharpened the miasma of hopelessness that generally hung around the mansion. The excited tension was palpable, pulling the atmosphere until it felt so tight it might shatter.

Bartholomew was about to press the big red button. Quick and her friends were getting out just in time. She should be grateful for that.

And yet.

Kulika wasn't at the house, or in the block, or anywhere else on the property. As far as Quick could tell, Bartholomew wasn't either.

'Did you find her?' Evita asked when Quick returned to the suite at the house with her packed handbag.

'No. Did you?'

'No, but I found that little shit Monty,' said Evita. 'He said they went out, Kulika to do this formula thing and Bartholomew to go do whatever he does with his free time. Setting things on fire or torturing animals, probably.'

'Without even saying goodbye?' Quick said. It came out as a whine.

'Probably to avoid it, definitely in Bartholomew's case,' Evita said bitterly. 'He knows that if I ever get my hands on him I'm going to fucking murder him.' She gathered up her own meagre possessions and said, 'Home, then.'

'Home,' Quick repeated.

The word felt unaccountably big.

Their cab was late.

Quick kept thinking it was fate, that Kulika would come rushing around the corner at any second to sweep her up in elaborate goodbyes and promises of being reunited in future, or maybe she'd even ask to come with them back to the UK. They were childish fantasies, she knew, but she wished them true anyway.

Of course Kulika hadn't come. Other people had, though: Penny, Brandon, and other Silver Evita knew from her days at the mansion whom Quick had never met. They didn't seem to come out of fondness, but more out of boredom, inebriation, and a vague fascination about whatever had happened to make Bartholomew release them from his covenant.

They were all gone now, though, back to their party. The

cab was twenty minutes late and Quick was sitting under her parasol on the mansion's front steps with Evita, looking out onto the drive as they waited for it to arrive. They'd all had to pick new clothes out of the wardrobe at the block so they'd have something to wear that wasn't dirty and covered in holes. Quick had dug out a copper-coloured, long-sleeved cotton dress and Evita had found some jeans and a T-shirt that fitted her, which was easier at her size. Quick just had to take what she could get. They each had a small bag of items with them too, the scavenged remnants of what they'd brought to this place, and they were lucky to have that. Xiaoyu had nothing at all.

The only human in their party had been nervous all morning. She wanted to look as nice as she could for her return home. As they'd been sitting there in the sunshine waiting for their ride, she'd seen a speck of blood on her inherited jeans and rushed to the mansion's bathroom to rinse it off. She didn't want her kids to see it.

It seemed like whatever they did, blood would follow them. Unfortunately, Quick and Evita still needed it to survive, a fact Quick was trying her hardest to ignore. They were already painfully underfed. Quick had maybe one or two short bursts of speed left in her, but Evita had nothing in the tank at all. She'd used everything they'd given her just to heal her wounds.

'We might have to grab someone in the airport before we leave,' Evita murmured the moment Xiaoyu left for the bathroom. 'For the blood.'

Quick gave her a horrified look.

'I know, okay?' Evita continued. 'But if we touch down in the UK blood-starved like this, and if Bartholomew's already done his grand revelation, we might have to fight our way through on the other side. A pair of sunglasses isn't going to fool people for long once they know to look for the silver in our eyes, and when they see your parasol' – Evita flicked the handle – 'people are going to get suspicious.'

'And your solution is to attack someone at the airport? Don't you think that'll make people even more suspicious?'

'Not if we do it carefully. In the bathrooms, maybe, when no one else is around.'

Quick considered the offhand way Evita was talking and the fact that she already had a plan, and came to a conclusion she didn't much like.

'You've done this before,' Quick said.

Evita was quiet for so long that Quick began to regret the accusation in her words.

'I didn't mean to—'

'Do you know that one of the most effective ways for cults to brainwash their members is by limiting their food intake?' Evita interrupted. At first it sounded like a non sequitur, but then she continued: 'It makes people more suggestible. When you don't get enough food – or blood – then your brain starts weakening along with your body. Then, just when you're starting to feel that weakness, they start working you like they worked us back at the block. They get you to do manual labour, or to run laps or fight or whatever. Combine that with a starvation diet of high-carb food, and weird things start happening. You get periods of complete euphoria followed by crushing misery, apparently for no reason at all. You're so tired that you can't think straight, so you don't put two and two together. Maybe they pair you up with some hottie, someone who's all-in on whatever the cult's doctrine is, so you don't notice the craziness of it because the words are coming from a face you wouldn't mind waking up next to.'

Quick knew whose face that was for her, but it made her

wonder about Evita.

'The outrageous starts to sound reasonable,' Evita continued. 'In that state, you do things you would never even have contemplated previously, awful things, so if you ever do surface for brief moments of lucidity, you want to dive right back into the depths of your delusion just so it can all make sense again. You're not a bad person, it's just that terrible things are necessary in the cult's reality, so you cling to that reality like a lifeline. You can't accept any challenge to it, because if you do then all your excuses will shatter along with the world that's been constructed around you, and suddenly you have to look yourself in the eye and admit the truth: not only are you not a good person, you're just someone else's pawn.'

Who'd convinced her to do terrible things, and what exactly had she done?

'What are you telling me?' Quick asked.

'I was here for months before you arrived,' Evita replied. 'You've barely been here a week. All I'm saying is: don't judge me for doing what I had to do to keep my head above water. And if I have to do it again, for both of us, then I will.'

Xiaoyu returned then, putting an end to the conversation before Quick could smooth things over. It made the atmosphere awkward, which wasn't helped by the fact that she felt more self-conscious around Xiaoyu now, particularly after what had happened with Brandon this morning. When Quick had told him they were taking Xiaoyu with them when they left, he'd said, *Little snack for the journey?*

Evita had punched him, right in the face. She had a right hook that would make Kulika proud.

Kulika.

Quick didn't need that intrusive echo in her already muddled mind, so she pushed the thought away. In much the same way Kulika had pushed *her* away: mercilessly, and with determined finality.

It was time that Quick did the same, and turned her mind to the future instead.

'Do you think they'll let us have our old jobs back?' she asked Evita. She was over a week late coming back from her sabbatical at this point, but she had to believe the university would give her a little leeway on that, particularly since she would be returning with their star historian in tow.

'Do you think they'll willingly employ vampires once Bartholomew drags us all out into the open?' Evita asked bluntly.

'Probably not,' said Xiaoyu.

'I guess that's the end of our academic lives, then,' said Quick.

'I don't know,' said Evita. 'Bartholomew told me one of the Oxford colleges is mostly Silver.'

'Oh?'

'Solomon College.'

Quick thought hard, trying to remember if she'd ever met anyone who tutored there. It was part of the job when you were a university lecturer – circulate around the conferences, network with other professionals in your field, read their papers – so she recognised most of the colleges and universities in the UK, at least the ones that had a history faculty. But Solomon College wasn't ringing any bells.

'Yeah,' said Evita. 'I'd never heard of it either.'

The car finally arrived, and they all piled inside. No one came to wave them off. Quick stared out of the window as they circled the drive, her eyes fixed on the mansion's front door, imagining in vain that Kulika might be somewhere inside, that she might run out to stop the car before they left. As they started down the long road to the highway, Quick turned in her seat to look out of the back window, her eyes scanning the house until it was swallowed up by the oaks and Spanish moss that hung over the drive.

'I'm sorry,' Evita murmured, taking her hand.

'She didn't come,' Quick whispered back.

'We're free, though,' Evita replied. 'Isn't that better?'

Quick forced a smile onto her face and squeezed Evita's hand, pretending that she agreed. Evita smiled back, apparently convinced.

If only Quick could convince herself as easily as she could convince her best friend.

4

KULIKA DROVE BARTHOLOMEW'S stupid little sports car too fast around the corners, willing it to roll. She'd like to see it dented. She'd like to smash it to pieces, scratch up the paint and shatter the headlights. She wouldn't be hurt, not in the long run, but Bartholomew would certainly be angry if she stained his cream leather seats with her blood. She'd like to see that, too.

I couldn't help it, she'd say. *Someone was driving on the wrong side of the road, coming the other way. I had to spin off the road to avoid hitting them.*

He couldn't punish her for that, could he?

It was a petty rebellion, but she'd get to watch a little piece of his soul getting crushed by the loss, and that would be worth her pain. For the pain he'd caused her, she'd suffer the same all over again if it would cause him even the tiniest discomfort.

But there were always more cars. He wouldn't have lent her this one if he cared much for it; it wasn't as though the thing was irreplaceable. Not like a person. Not like Quick.

She cut the speed. As rebellions went, it wouldn't just be petty, it would be pointless as well. Quick would be gone by the time she returned to the mansion, and that was for the best. Bartholomew was right about that, for all that Kulika hated him for it. It was time she put Quick behind her and concentrated on the people she could still help: her crew, Jack bloody Valentine, and Baron Drake.

She drove carefully the rest of the way to the lab, watching her speed the whole time.

When Kulika walked in through the security doors, Dr Ross had her glasses in one hand and was rubbing her eyes with the other. At first, Kulika thought she must be tired – after all, she'd stayed up all night to work on the formula – but when the doctor took her hand away to look at Kulika, her eyes were wet with tears.

'It didn't work,' Dr Ross said.

Kulika stopped dead in the doorway. 'What didn't work?' she asked stupidly. She already knew, she just didn't want it to be true.

'Evita Khalyed's blood isn't close enough to Jahan Khalyed's. The formula doesn't behave the same way in her blood as it did in his. It's not bonding, it's just burning through it, like it does with all the other Silver.'

'Which means?'

'I can't replicate the toxin that's poisoning Jack,' Dr Ross said hopelessly. 'And if I can't replicate it, I can't make an antidote. Jack Valentine is going to die.'

Kulika sat down heavily onto the nearest chair. 'And Baron Drake along with her,' she said.

Dr Ross nodded, wiping her eyes again.

Once upon a time, Dr Ross had been almost as close to Jack Valentine as Baron Drake was now. She might pretend she was crying for the baron, but they both knew her tears were really for her former flame. Kulika felt like crying too.

It had all been for nothing.

She'd come to South Carolina in search of Evita Khalyed. She'd walked back into Bartholomew's mansion, a place she'd hoped never to see again, all so she could find Evita, so Dr Ross could make an antidote for Jack. Kulika had done *everything* right. She'd discovered what had happened to Evita, tracked her down – with no help from Job Bayly – rescued her, and secured a sample of her blood. She'd even negotiated a place for Dr Ross to do her work in Enzo's lab at BioSilver, and it had all come to nothing. All that effort on a gamble that hadn't paid off.

And now she was bound to Bartholomew again, more tightly than ever, with nothing to show for it but a love she would never see requited.

For a moment, the two of them were silent, then Dr Ross took a deep, shuddering breath and settled her glasses back on her nose.

'I need to call him,' she said. 'Maybe I can bring the blood samples back with me and fiddle with them in the lab a bit, maybe fudge a little, but it's a slim chance and… But maybe…' She was procrastinating, Kulika could tell. She didn't blame the doctor for that. She didn't like giving bad news to the baron either, and it couldn't get much worse than, *You and the woman you love are both going to die*.

'I'll call him,' said Kulika. 'He should… He'll want to hear it from me, and you need to get back to Oxford. He'll need you. Besides, things are happening here at the mansion, and I'm not sure I…' She trailed off.

'Kulika?' Dr Ross asked, but Kulika didn't know how to finish the sentence.

She was unsure of so much, but what she couldn't admit to Dr Ross was the one thing of which she was completely certain: Bartholomew was about to unleash hell on earth, and he was going to use Kulika to do it.

In the end, Kulika just said, 'You should go.'

Dr Ross was already packing up her things. 'You'll tell Baron Drake that I'll keep trying?'

'I will.'

The doctor unzipped an insulated carrying case that had space inside for six tubes. She stowed five in the padded holders, then looked at Kulika expectantly. 'Did you find my missing vial?'

In all the commotion of the past day, Kulika hadn't thought to call Dr Ross about the trouble with Bella, and the vial. She'd just left her to get on with her work.

'We did,' Kulika said quietly. 'But not until it was too late.'

'Oh, god.' The doctor sat back down again, face in her hands. She looked up at Kulika through her fingers and asked, 'Who died?'

'One of the newer Silver from Bartholomew's crew. No one else.' Kulika paused. 'At least, not exactly.'

Dr Ross dropped her hands, gave Kulika a blank look for a moment, then said, 'Explain.'

So Kulika told Dr Ross what Bartholomew had told her last night: about Bella's experiment with the zombies, and how instead of having one normal failed-turning zombie, they now had seven super zombies who were apparently indestructible.

'How is that possible?' Dr Ross asked when Kulika was finished.

'I don't know. Bartholomew's been testing them and… Well, I took his word for it.'

'I suppose it makes sense,' the doctor said thoughtfully. 'After all, when Jahan Khalyed took the serum, it made him insatiably hungry for Silver blood. If it's putting the same hunger in the zombies… The resilience, though. That's new.

But not entirely, maybe,' she murmured, talking to herself now. 'After all, the formula makes most Silver burn up to nothing, and when Dr Jay bit the Silver, his victims did exactly that, so maybe there's some inheritance of the formula that passes to the carrier in the same way that... Hmm.'

'Dr Ross?'

'I want to see them,' she said, getting to her feet and smoothing down her skirts. 'If this is a side effect of the formula, then I need to know about it. It might help with the antidote. If I took a sample of their blood—'

'I'll get you one. Just book yourself on a flight—'

'The Baron sent me in his plane. It's waiting for me at Charleston.'

'Then wait here, and I'll be back in an hour.'

The doctor gave Kulika a level look.

'You want to go back to the mansion, don't you?' Kulika asked hopelessly.

'Yes.'

'But you know how dangerous he is. I'm already stuck here. I don't want you to get stuck too. The baron needs you.'

'He needs *you*,' the doctor said.

'Then don't risk him losing both of us at once.'

'We're going to lose *him* if I can't get to the bottom of this antidote. Please, Kulika,' she said, looking pleadingly into her eyes. 'If there's a chance that I could learn something from them, I have to go, whatever the risk. You understand that, don't you?'

Kulika did, all too well. It was the reason she'd walked back into the mansion in the first place, even though she'd known in her heart of hearts that she would never freely walk out again.

'Have you got all the other vials?' Kulika said, eyeing the doctor's bench carefully.

'Yes,' Dr Ross said, stowing the padded bag inside her doctor's bag. 'And don't worry: I've got all the waste products in here too. I'm not leaving anything behind for BioSilver to find.'

'Good,' said Kulika. 'Then let's go.'

'Thank you,' the doctor started saying, but then Kulika's phone buzzed in her pocket, at the same time as the landline on Enzo's desk started chirping.

'Yeah?' Kulika said as she answered, surprised to see that the call was from Bayly's number. She wasn't sure what Bartholomew had done with her old crew-mate, but she was relieved to see the name pop up on her phone.

Except he wasn't the one making the call.

'They got out,' a panicked voice said on the other end of the line.

'What got... Penny? Is that you?'

'The zombies. The weird ones we took off Bella,' she said. 'They got out and...' Her voice was hushed and shrill at the same time, and in the background Kulika could hear screaming. A lot of screaming. Somewhere in the distance, a siren was blaring, then another, and another, and they couldn't be coming from the mansion because Kulika knew Bartholomew didn't have an alarm system, for fire or security or anything else.

'Where's Quick?' Kulika asked. 'Did she get to the airport all right?'

'They got a cab,' said Penny. 'They were already gone by the time we noticed the first zombie in the trees, then we saw the wine cellar was open, and...'

'But you caught the zombies, right?'

'One of them. The others...'

'You're Silver,' Kulika said impatiently. 'They're zombies. This isn't difficult. You can move a hundred times faster than them.'

'Not *all* of them,' Penny insisted. 'There's… They just… We're not supposed to go down there,' she trailed off hopelessly. 'And the things that got out, they're not *normal*.'

'Where's Bartholomew?'

'Still sailing. That's why we're calling you.'

Kulika locked eyes with Dr Ross for a moment. It was clear from the doctor's expression that she could hear everything that was happening on the other end of the line.

The doctor said, 'We're coming.'

When Kulika screeched Bartholomew's sports car to a halt on the driveway outside the mansion, Penny was already waiting.

'They were down in the wine cellar,' she said, leading the way to the kitchen at the back of the mansion. 'Monty told us to chain them up, and then the cap— the Primus came in and was… I don't know.'

'What were the sirens?' Kulika asked.

'They were in the block. There was a fire.'

'Another one?'

'It's fine. It's out now, and anyway: one disaster at a time, right? It's down here,' Penny said, crossing the kitchen to the wine cellar's door.

'I know,' Kulika replied.

Bartholomew had taken her down into the unnatural cold of that cellar to see Cara Alton's body. That was before he'd sent it off to be displayed for the creepy jogger who'd taken her photos. She wouldn't soon forget the atmosphere of the place, or the smell. It was worse now, though: thick and bloody and sweet to the point that it smelled rancid.

'I recognise that smell,' Dr Ross said, hesitating at the top of the brick stairs as Penny held the door open for them.

'Blood?' Kulika asked.

'Dead things,' the doctor said.

'How many were down here?' Kulika asked Penny.

'All of them. All seven.'

'How many got out?'

'At least two,' Penny said. 'We saw them running across the lawn.'

'You haven't gone down to check?' Kulika asked, angrily pointing at the cellar. 'Don't you think maybe that should have been the first thing you did?'

'We didn't think— That is, with what the Primus was keeping down there…'

'Where's everyone else?' Dr Ross asked.

'Over at the block, or out searching. Monty's organising them. But I don't think you understand,' Penny said, turning back to Kulika. 'There's something *else* down there.'

'What?'

But Penny just shook her head, looking like she was genuinely scared. That didn't add up. It was enough to hurry Kulika's steps down into the cellar, with Dr Ross hot on her heels.

There was blood. That was the first thing Kulika noticed; it would have been hard to miss. It started in a pool at the foot of the stairs, then spattered up the walls and the stone plinth in the centre of the room and ran in tacky streams along the walls. There was so much of it that it took Kulika a while to see what she was actually looking at.

'Christ alive,' the doctor muttered, standing on the bottom step beside Kulika as they both stared down into the pool beneath them.

It was moving.

When Kulika adjusted her perception with that in mind,

she finally saw that the pool wasn't as shallow as it had first appeared. In fact it was nearly half a foot deep, filling the part of the uneven cellar floor that sloped down towards the base of the stairwell.

And there were… *things* in it.

'I count three skulls,' the doctor whispered.

'Zombies?' Kulika asked her.

'That would be my guess. If they were Silver, they would be healing, and if they were human—'

'They'd be dead.'

'Right.'

But whatever they were, they were definitely not dead, or at least not inanimate. Pieces of what had once been people bobbed and dipped in the puddle of gore, moving in a fluid way that seemed impossible for such dissected things.

'Do you want to take your blood samples from that?' Kulika asked, pointing towards the writhing pool, but then her attention was caught by a noise on the other side of the cellar. 'Wait here,' she said to the doctor, then she leapt up onto the plinth to get clear of the blood pooling on the floor.

Which would have been an excellent idea, had the plinth still been sealed. Unfortunately, the lid was now lying smashed on the floor, hidden from view from the doorway by the plinth itself. Instead of landing neatly out of the blood, Kulika stumbled into the open casket and ended up on her knees inside it. There was a dark, viscous fluid smeared around the inner walls. When Kulika got to her feet, it was all over her hands, too.

It smelled familiar.

'Are you all right?' the doctor asked.

Then Kulika heard the noise again: a gravelly rasp, like the scraping of nail on stone. She had to peer around the corner of the alcove where Cara Alton's body had been before she could identify its source.

'Bayly?' Kulika said.

Like the puddle at the bottom of the stairs, at first she couldn't put together the objects in the alcove and form them into a figure. Eventually she realised that this was because there were two figures in the alcove, both Enzo and Bayly, curled together and bloodied. Neither of them was moving.

'Shit,' she muttered, jumping down from the plinth to the alcove.

Bayly was in pieces, quite literally. There were chunks of flesh missing from his calves, his upper arms, his stomach, and parts of him had been entirely removed: a finger, a toe, a knee cap. Worse, he wasn't healing, because the only blood he had left was what had been smeared over his skin. Wrapped in Bayly's arms, Enzo had been drained too, but not mutilated. From the way Bayly was curled around him, it looked as though Bayly had used his own body to shield Enzo from harm.

The gesture made the part of Kulika that missed Quick ache.

'Doctor, get over here please,' she said. 'I need your help.'

There was a gentle *thud* as Dr Ross leapt over the puddle of zombies, then she was standing at Kulika's side, her fingers pressing gently against Bayly's wrist to feel for a pulse.

'God, is this what Bartholomew does to his prisoners? This is torture.'

'Maybe,' Kulika said, 'but I don't think this was Bartholomew.'

'He's shut down,' the doctor said as she released Bayly's wrist. 'We're going to need to get him into a blood bath.'

'And the other?'

The doctor felt Enzo's wrist, then declared, 'Not so bad,

but we may as well put them in together. Assuming, that is…?'

'This one silvered for this one,' Kulika said, pointing between the two men. 'They're together.'

'Then they'll heal better if we keep them that way. Help me get them upstairs.'

Kulika held up her hands, showing the black goo to the doctor. 'I don't want to touch them with this,' she said.

'What *is* that?'

Now that she'd had a moment to think about it, and now that she'd seen the state of Bayly, Kulika had a pretty good idea. She recognised the strange sheen of it, and she could follow its trail to the outside corner of the cellar, where bricks had been pried up from the ground to form the entrance to a tunnel leading out.

Well, she supposed, they hadn't called him *Digs* for nothing. Bayly's ex had drunk enough Silver blood to put him back in action, and now he was loose.

5

QUICK WAS THOUGHTFUL and quiet on the drive as she watched the trees whipping by along the roadside.

First the cab was dropping her and Evita at the airport, then it would carry on into Charleston proper to take Xiaoyu home. It turned out that she was a local, despite her accent, the answer to yet another question Quick had never bothered to ask. Somehow, home addresses hadn't seemed like vital information when they'd been down in the blood cellar. Now, thinking of all the people they'd left behind there, and all the missing persons who'd disappeared into that mansion, Quick wondered if they should have been. She could have made lists. She might not have been able to save everyone, but she could at least have brought some answers back for the families who'd been searching for them.

It was too late now. Quick was leaving with nothing but a bruised heart and the guilt of having done so little when she'd had the chance.

The radio was on, full of reports about the discovery of Cara Alton's body and the strange silver marks on her skin. The passengers all exchanged a few looks at that, but they couldn't talk about it, not with the cab driver listening.

Instead, Xiaoyu and Evita chatted a little, getting to know each other. Quick didn't have much to say. She couldn't help but feel that she was making a mistake by leaving, abandoning all those people in the blood cellar to their fate, however shitty they'd been to Xiaoyu.

Quick was under no illusions about the fact that she'd sacrificed them all for the chance to get Evita and Xiaoyu out. That was something, though, wasn't it? Only…

Kulika.

'What I said about seductive hotties and cults,' Evita said quietly, reading Quick's mind as usual. 'I wasn't talking about you, you know. You might not understand Kulika's motives, but at least you can trust they were good ones.' Then she added lightly, 'You know she actually loves you.'

That shocked a laugh out of Quick. 'I don't know what gave you that idea.'

'She showed me her silver,' Evita said, fiddling with the strap of her bag. 'When she rescued me from that bastard box. I got all twitchy about her, and needed a reason to trust her, so she showed me her silver. It's all in the grey of her eyes.'

'I know,' Quick said, not following.

'So she's silvered for you,' Evita said, implying by her tone that she expected Quick to understand more from that statement than she in fact did.

Quick looked at her blankly. 'Okay,' she said. 'I'm still not following you.'

'Oh,' said Xiaoyu. 'Well, that explains a lot.' Then she leaned forward to look past Evita at Quick. 'You could have just told me,' she added. 'I wouldn't have told anyone.'

'Told anyone *what?*' Quick asked, looking between the two of them, bemused.

'Those silver marks that were on the back of your neck,'

Xiaoyu whispered. 'Kulika healed you, right? It was a handprint, like Cara Alton' – Xiaoyu mouthed the name – 'had on her stomach.'

'It was a—' Quick cut herself off, because suddenly she couldn't find the words.

The silver marks at her neck, from where Kulika bit her.

The silver at the roots of her hair, from where Kulika had held her as she'd saved her life.

The distant look in Kulika's eyes as she'd said goodbye last night, before Quick had even realised it *was* goodbye, a look that had burned into Quick's brain, and that she now recognised as barely-suppressed pain.

'It means she loves you,' Evita whispered. 'It's what gives her the power to heal you. Christ, Quick, are you telling me you didn't *know*?'

'No!' Quick yelled, loudly enough that the taxi pulled over in a scream of brakes.

'Hey,' said the driver solicitously, turning in her seat. 'You all right, there, baby girl? Damn near jumped out of my skin up here.'

'Sorry,' Quick said. 'I'm sorry, I didn't… Sorry. Just…'

'She's had a bit of a shock,' Evita explained.

Quick dropped her head between her knees. She couldn't breathe. She didn't actually *need* to breathe anymore, but it was a habit that was proving difficult for her body to break.

'Oh, god,' she said.

'Did she not tell you what it means?' Evita asked. 'It means—'

'Just give me a minute,' Quick said. Her brain felt like it had frozen.

'Do you want to go back?' Evita asked gently.

'Fuck, no,' said Xiaoyu. 'I'm not going back there. Not ever. Not if you paid me a million dollars.'

'Er,' Evita said uncertainly. 'You might want to drop that number a little. A lot, actually.'

'What's this, now?' the driver asked wonderingly. 'They making a zombie movie out here?'

Quick lifted her head and leaned over Evita into the centre of the back seat so she could see out of the windscreen. There were three figures walking down the centre of the road. Shambling, really. Quick recognised the one out in front.

Evita leaned forward. 'Is that—'

'That's one of the guys we brought back with Bella,' Quick said, her stomach dropping. 'The ones she turned zombie when she was out on her little frolic.'

'The ones who—'

'Don't die. And we've got two humans here. Back up,' Quick said urgently, but their driver hadn't grasped the urgency of the situation. 'Back up!' she yelled again, but by now it was too late: the zombies had already reached the car, and before Quick could even undo her seatbelt, Bella's zombie had smashed his fist through the driver's side window and was dragging their driver out by her throat. Quick grabbed her and tried to pull her back inside while she made a terrible noise somewhere between a scream and a gurgle, but the zombie pulled harder. Their driver was out on the road before either Evita or Xiaoyu had moved.

For a moment, there was no sound at all except the gentle purr of the engine as the car rolled forward, then their driver was back on her feet again, eyes bleeding and teeth bared, reaching back through the broken window towards Xiaoyu.

In the space of a second or less, their driver had turned into a zombie.

'Shit!' Quick yelled, then she scrambled over the centre console at Silver speed, slipping into the driver's seat. Their erstwhile driver reared back, giving Quick just enough time to slam her foot on the accelerator and jerk the car forward down the road.

'Christ,' Xiaoyu said from the back seat. 'What the fuck was that?'

'You saw that, right?' Quick asked incredulously.

'I saw a zombie bite a human and turn her into one of their own,' Xiaoyu said as the car sped along. 'But that's just science fiction. Real zombies don't do that.'

'They do now,' Evita said.

'Bella gave hers some kind of potion,' Quick said, taking the next turn fast enough that two of the car's wheels lifted off the road for a heart-thudding moment before slamming back down again. 'Maybe it didn't just make them indestructible. Maybe it made them infectious, too.'

'Shit,' said Xiaoyu. 'But if they infect any human they bite, and then that human infects any human *they* bite…'

'It's like the world's shittest game of dominoes,' said Quick.

'And they're all after me,' Xiaoyu said darkly.

It was a reasonable assumption: she was the only human left in the car.

Quick took another corner that sent the sunshine streaming in through the broken driver's side window, and before she'd even noticed the danger, her left arm was on fire.

'Shit!' she screamed, pulling her arm close against her body to try to extinguish the flames. Her foot slammed on the brake, but the pedal wasn't quite where she'd expected it to be, and she only succeeded in slowing the car briefly before her foot slid off. By that point, Evita had reached over the back of Quick's chair and thrown her jacket over the steering wheel, effectively quenching the fire.

'Shit,' Quick winced. The flames were gone, but the burning pain they'd left in their wake was enough to have Quick blinking back tears.

'Pull over,' Evita ordered. 'I'll drive.'

'No,' Quick insisted. 'I'm fine. Just…' She fumbled her feet around on the foot pedals until she found the accelerator, then they were off again. 'I'm fine.'

'I'm not,' Xiaoyu muttered. 'Holy shit.'

'I thought the zombies were locked up,' Evita said.

'So did I,' Quick replied, accidentally putting the car into park when she tried to change down for the next corner. She fumbled with the gearstick. 'Shit,' she said. 'I keep forgetting this is an automatic.'

'So pull over and let me drive,' Evita said again.

'I said I'm fine,' Quick bit out. 'Anyway, I can't get out of the car to change seats. I'll burn to death out there.'

'We don't have to get out of the car,' Evita argued.

'She said she's fine,' Xiaoyu said, with unexpected gentleness. That was enough to calm Quick down a little, then everything got easier.

Eventually, Quick got the car back into drive, but she still kept thumping an invisible clutch with her foot as they sped along, trying to change gears. She didn't have anywhere to put her left foot and she kept hitting the brake and the accelerator at the same time. She risked taking a split-second to peek into the footwell so she could work out where the pedals actually were, and in that split-second everything went wrong again.

'Quick!' Evita yelled from the back seat, then something hit the front of the car. Quick slammed on the brakes, but Xiaoyu was yelling, 'Drive! Drive!'

The windscreen cleared with a thump that sent something flying off to one side of the road. It was a body, Quick realised. She'd hit someone. Oh god, she'd hit someone.

Then she saw exactly what she'd hit, and she had to blink to make sure she wasn't seeing things.

'Drive!' Xiaoyu yelled again.

On the grass verge by the side of the road, a woman was getting to her feet. She wasn't alone, though. Melting out of the darkness between the tress, there were more of them. A *lot* more of them. There were people in every state of dress and undress, some of them scratched and muddy, all of them bloodstained, and some so badly injured that it made Quick squeamish even to look at them. She couldn't imagine how they were still walking on legs that looked twisted and broken, and with gashes across their torsos that spilled out things that really should have stayed tucked away inside. Their injuries were as varied as they were numerous, but they shared one common wound: every single one of them was crying bloody tears from red eyes.

They were crowding towards the car now, blocking the road right across its width. Quick worked the gearstick clumsily, and the car sped back the way they'd come, in reverse.

'Shit shit shit,' she muttered.

'Turn around!' Evita yelled.

'Don't turn around!' Xiaoyu yelled. 'They must have come from the mansion. We can't go back there!'

'Well we can't go through here either!' Evita yelled.

In the end, their argument was academic. Unseen by any of them, a large pick-up truck had barrelled around the bend behind them going twice the speed limit – doubtless trying to escape the zombies – and slammed right into the back of their car, pitching it off the side of the road and into the trees. The two vehicles rolled down the highway embankment together for twenty yards or so before finally coming to rest in a steaming, mangled pile of metal in a stream at the bottom of a scar they'd carved through the forest.

Up on the road, a hundred broken people turned in the direction of the crash. Following the vehicles, or seeing the smoke, or attracted by the noise, or maybe even scenting blood – who knows what goes on in a zombie's head? – they ran.

6

KULIKA HAD WASHED her hands thoroughly and was now helping the doctor to carry the unwieldy, curled-up bodies of Bayly and Enzo up the staircase to the bathroom on the first floor. She'd tried calling Bartholomew before they'd moved the pair, but she kept getting an error message. Wherever he'd taken the ship for his test sail, apparently it was out of network range.

'Why was Digs even in the cellar?' Kulika asked Penny irritably. 'I left him on Bayly's boat for a reason. He was locked up tight.'

'I don't know,' Penny replied.

'Did he get loose and follow us here, or did someone put him down there?'

'I don't know,' Penny said again.

'Well you must know *something*.' Kulika was quickly getting exasperated. Penny was the most senior Silver left at the mansion, they couldn't get hold of anyone else on their phones, and she knew absolutely nothing of use.

'Where are you holding the one zombie you caught?' Kulika asked, not expecting a helpful reply.

'In the back of the truck parked on the driveway,' Penny

49

said. 'We locked it in. We couldn't think of anywhere else to put it.'

'We're going to need blood,' the doctor said. 'A lot of blood. Do you have bottles?'

'No,' Penny said.

Dr Ross gave her a quizzical look.

'Bartholomew makes them all drink from the vein,' Kulika explained. 'No bottles or bags at the mansion.'

'What?' the doctor asked. 'Why?'

'It's a pirate thing,' Kulika said. 'A stupid pirate thing,' she added.

Kulika hated the blood cellar. She hated taking blood from people who didn't want to give it, and she hated that Bartholomew had made it so that the crew had no other choice. She'd do it, though. To save her crew, she would do anything that was necessary, but she could at least minimise the harm caused by the process.

She turned to Penny. 'Bleed some donors from the blood cellar. You're going to need a lot of them, because I only want you to take a little from each, and only from the ones who can spare it. Be careful, too; I'm going to be checking on them later to make sure you were.'

She was expecting Penny to snap to it, but the redhead was still trailing along behind them. They were on the landing now, shuffling along the corridor to the bathroom, and there wasn't enough space for Penny to walk alongside.

'What?' Kulika asked.

'It's just… When the Primus comes home and sees that Bayly and Enzo are out of the wine cellar—'

'Bartholomew can give whatever orders he wants when he's here. When he's not, I'm in charge. Is that understood?'

'Yes, okay.'

'Get the blood and get back here, and I want a report from

the search parties. Send someone to find them. And get Monty up here, too. We need to find Digs, and we need to do it now.'

Penny hurried off with another murmured, 'Yes, okay,' leaving Kulika and the doctor to manoeuvre Bayly and Enzo through the bathroom doorway and gently lower them into the clawfoot bathtub.

'They don't seem very organised,' Dr Ross commented.

'They're not.' Kulika sighed, pushing her hair back from her face. 'They can't look after themselves. I did try to warn Bartholomew. The problem is, they're all so young.'

'The problem is,' the doctor countered, 'what he's doing here is utter madness. It's dangerous, it's uncontrolled, and it's only going to get worse. Tell me you realise that.'

'I'm trying my best to manage it,' Kulika said helplessly. 'That's all I can do.'

'You could leave.'

'No,' Kulika said. 'Not without hurting Quick. At least she's safe now.'

'With what he has planned, I don't think any of us are *safe*,' the doctor muttered, then she turned her attention to the men lying in the bathtub. She sighed. 'Right. Let's get them as clean as we can before we soak them. Help me turn them?'

Thank god that the bath had a shower attachment, because without that there would have been no chance of rinsing the dirty blood from the bodies of the entwined men. As the filth washed away, the true extent of Bayly's injuries became clear. Just as he had done back on the boat at the marina, Digs had bitten chunks out of Bayly's flesh. Kulika could see the teeth marks.

'Tell me again about Digs,' Dr Ross asked as she leaned in closer to examine one of the bites.

'He was a pirate who got locked in a box for more than three hundred years,' said Kulika. 'That's about all I know.'

'Hmm.' The doctor muttered a sentence or two to herself, but Kulika couldn't make out the words. Then she said, 'This isn't the first time a Silver has been locked in a box for decades, centuries even. It's normal for them to come out thirsty, but they don't usually start eating chunks of other Silvers' flesh.'

'They do often lose their minds, though,' Kulika pointed out.

'True. Maybe that's all this is. I certainly *hope* that's all it is.'

'Why? What are you thinking?'

Dr Ross pursed her lips for a moment, as though she was considering whether or not to voice her suspicions at all.

Kulika raised her eyebrows.

'It's just a theory,' the doctor said. 'Not even a theory, just a thought, really. I don't want to set hares running if it's all in my head, but I think there is a possibility that he's been contaminated by the zombies in the wine cellar. Either way, we'd better find him, and quickly.'

'Contaminated how?' Penny said, returning to the room.

'Long story,' said Kulika.

'Contaminated *how*?' Penny insisted. 'I touched those zombies. We all did. Are we going to get contaminated too and turn into… that?'

'No, it's…' Dr Ross said. 'It's complicated.' The doctor looked down at the floor for a moment, arranging her thoughts before launching into the explanation. 'About twenty years ago – longer, even – there was a doctor who worked for Solomon's research department in Oxford, a man named Dr Jahan Khalyed. He was trying to develop a formula that would prevent the Silver from needing to drink human blood. A philanthropic endeavour. Laudable, I think you'll agree.'

'Stupid,' Kulika said. 'Because it went wrong.'

Dr Ross sighed and said, 'Yes, it went wrong. After a little self-experimentation, he started biting other Silver in a semi-conscious state that he couldn't control. Every time he bit another Silver, some part of the formula transferred to them through his saliva, and they just… burned up. In flames. The same way that the unadulterated formula kills most Silver. Eventually, we had to imprison Jahan, for his own safety and the safety of everyone else.'

'But?' Penny asked.

'But someone—'

'Jack Valentine,' Kulika supplied helpfully. Perhaps spitefully.

'Yes,' Dr Ross grudgingly agreed, 'Jack broke into his cell and stole some of Jahan's blood, intending to use it to kill the Primus, Solomon.'

'Would that have worked?' Penny asked, wide-eyed.

'Probably,' Dr Ross said. 'Yes. On its own, the formula Jahan created is only strong enough to kill younger or weaker Silver.'

'But it didn't kill Jahan?' Penny asked, confused.

'No. He had a kind of immunity to it. When combined with Jahan's blood, the formula… mutates, is the easiest way to explain it. Instead of burning through his body like it would with most other Silver, the formula bonded to Jahan's blood to become an incredibly potent poison. That's what Jack hoped to use to kill the Primus.'

'But this Jack didn't succeed, right?' Penny asked.

'No, of course not,' Kulika said. 'She's an idiot.'

'Yes,' Dr Ross agreed again. 'Sometimes she is. Jack managed to smash the vial of Jahan's infected blood, and accidentally infected herself with a tiny drop of the poison, which is now killing her slowly. I've been working on an antidote, but I can't make one without replicating the original poison, and I can't do that without Jahan's blood. But, due to a very unfortunate series of circumstances that I won't go into right now, there's none left. I came here to take a blood sample from Evita – Jahan's last living descendant – in the hopes that I might be able to combine it with the original formula Jahan took in order to recreate the poison and manufacture an antidote to it. Unsuccessfully, unfortunately.'

This was all old news to Kulika.

'Can we get back to the contamination theory, please?' she asked impatiently.

The doctor sucked her bottom lip anxiously for a moment, then said, 'The thing is, I have a concern.'

'Which is?' Kulika asked.

Dr Ross fiddled with the coffee stirrer that was still valiantly keeping her hair in place, then said, 'When Jahan turned into... whatever he turned into, he stopped craving human blood at all. That was his intention, of course, but there were unintended side effects. Instead of human blood, he started biting the Silver.'

'Like Digs bit Bayly,' Kulika said in a hollow voice, looking at Bayly's mutilated body in the bath tub.

'Precisely. This is my concern: *if* Evita's blood has indeed inherited the same traits that made Jahan immune to the formula, and *if* Digs drank enough of it while they were in that box together for it to affect his own immunity, and *if* he then drank enough blood from the zombies in the cellar – who had ingested the formula – that he has himself effectively ingested the formula, *then* it is possible that he has become the same kind of creature that Jahan once became.'

'You mean, someone who's immune to the formula?' Penny asked.

'I mean a zombie vampire who incinerates everyone he bites.'

Shit.

Kulika was silent for a moment, assessing all the weapons at her disposal in the mansion and finding them wanting against a mutated Silver who could kill them with a single bite.

'But we know that Evita's blood isn't the same as Jahan's was,' Kulika said. 'Your tests proved that. And Bayly didn't actually die when Digs bit him. Didn't you say the Silver that Jahan bit went up in smoke?'

'Yes, I did,' the doctor said. 'And those are about the only things that are giving me hope right now, but it's not black and white. With all these volatile substances combining and interacting, there's a possibility that Digs has become something else entirely.'

'I don't know,' Kulika said. 'It all sounds a little far-fetched to me. Seems more likely he just lost his marbles.'

'Well, I certainly hope you're right, because if that's true, then we can kill him with this,' the doctor said, patting the cool bag that held the vials of her formula. She was wearing it across her body, unwilling to let it out of her sight.

'And if we can't?' Penny asked.

'Then we box him, again,' said Kulika. 'This time for good. Where's the blood for Bayly?' Kulika demanded, only now noticing that Penny had arrived empty-handed. 'Where's Monty?'

'Still out searching,' said Penny. 'I've sent some of the newbies out looking, but we can't find him yet, or Brandon.'

'What about the older crew members?' Kulika asked. 'The

Silver who were here at the Convocation, and who were here this morning at the river? Why is the mansion suddenly empty?'

'They went with Bartholomew on the ship, or off site to prepare for tonight. And it gets worse.'

Kulika groaned. 'We've got three missing zombies and a bloodthirsty, centuries old, possibly cannibalistic Silver on the loose, plus half the crew is missing. How does that get worse?'

'The blood cellar's empty,' Penny whispered.

'What?' Kulika yelled. 'There were a hundred people down there!'

'More,' Penny admitted. 'We were busy setting things up for this evening, and then—'

'You mean you were busy partying.' Kulika gave Penny a stern look, and the woman crumpled.

'They must have got out while we were putting out the fire, then we found out the door to the wine cellar was open, and everything got busy,' Penny said desperately, her voice rising in pitch as she went on. 'And I tried to find the others, but I'm not the best tracker, which is why I'm still here, and honestly? I'm scared. I'm nervous about this evening, I feel sick ever since Bartholomew left the property this morning, like I can't even think straight, and now that the rest of the crew has gone off and left me here—'

'Okay,' said Dr Ross, gathering Penny's hands into her own. 'Okay, deep breaths.'

Penny was going to pieces. Less literally than Bayly, true, but she was going to be about as much use as he was right now.

'Can you handle this?' Kulika asked Dr Ross quietly.

She nodded back. 'Go find Digs and the others. We can't do much for these two without blood,' she added, glancing towards the bathtub. 'I've got a few of bottles of my own in my bag downstairs. Take what you need, and we'll use the rest to do what we can here.'

'All right.' Kulika was already heading for the stairs. 'And if you still want samples from those zombies,' she called back to the doctor, 'then get them now. I'm calling the baron, and you're going to the airport as soon as I get back.'

At least that would put Dr Ross out of harm's way, and give them a chance of salvaging an antidote from what had otherwise been a complete failure of a mission. Kulika tallied it up in her head as she ran to the car.

Antidote: nope.

Quick: gone.

Kulika: bound to Bartholomew.

Collateral damage: three indestructible zombies, one blood-starved vampire, and over a hundred formerly-captive humans on the loose together in the woods.

What a mess.

If only the newly-turned Silver that comprised the rest of her crew weren't so completely useless. Kulika sighed. If she wanted this done properly, she was going to have to do it her own damn self.

Kulika made the call on speaker as she drove, which would have been easier if her phone hadn't been sliding around on the passenger seat while she cornered hard on her frantic drive away from the mansion.

'Kulika,' he said on the second ring. 'Tell me you've got the antidote.'

'I haven't,' she yelled, hoping the baron would still hear her, despite the fact that her phone had slid down somewhere beside the centre console on the last turn. From his groan, she guessed he had.

'It gets worse,' she yelled. 'I'm sorry, but it didn't work.

And things have gone a bit… wrong here. Look, I'm sending Dr Ross back to you, and quickly. She can tell you about it, but I'm…'

'You're what?' the baron's voice asked through the muffled speaker.

'I've been delayed.'

'Indefinitely?'

'Yes.'

He groaned again. 'I'm so sorry, Kulika. I didn't mean to do this to you. I didn't mean to lose you, as well as—'

The call cut out then, which was just as well. Kulika was too focused to manage a sentimental goodbye, and that's what Baron Drake would have wanted. It was better this way. A hundred years of service, abruptly ended. And when Jack didn't get her antidote and met her inevitable end, that would be nearly five hundred years of his life, abruptly ended with hers.

It didn't seem fair, but then life wasn't fair. Kulika had never been under any illusions that it was otherwise. All she could hope was that she could gather everyone back to the mansion in time to salvage something from this mess.

She'd already searched the woods surrounding the property and found them empty. There were trails marking the low branches of trees and trampled through the underbrush, but it was difficult to tell whether they'd been made by zombies or humans or Silver; the tracks were muddled, and there was so much activity, without any clear trail to follow. One thing had been clear, though: all the tracks headed away from the river, in the direction of the highway. Figuring that she'd catch up quicker by car than she would on foot with only the single bottle of blood she'd nabbed from the doctor's bag to speed her along, she'd hopped back into Bartholomew's sports car and hit the road.

She rolled all the windows down, letting the air pour through the car as she drove, and breathed. There were so many scents that it was difficult to discern what was going on, so she concentrated on scanning the sides of the road instead, looking for dropped items, footprints or other marks of passage to point the way. She hadn't been driving long when something caught her attention. If it hadn't been for the smell, Kulika might have driven straight past.

Fear.

But not only that. Underneath the sharp, animal scent of terror, there was another aroma: fruit ripening in the sunshine, crisp water bursting out of hillside springs, beds of moss covered in sheets of autumn leaves.

Quick.

But she should be at the airport by now. Hell, she should be in the air, flying back home with her best friend at her side, safe from everything that was happening in this godforsaken corner of South Carolina, and everything that was about to happen.

That scent, though. Kulika would never mistake it for another.

She careened across the road and braked Bartholomew's fancy car so sharply that she could smell burning. Then she threw herself from the driver's seat, leaving the door hanging open behind her, and pelted down the embankment, following the dark path that had been gouged out of it by the descent of two vehicles going far too fast.

The pick-up truck had come to rest first, its bumper wedged tightly between two trees. The driver's side door was open, the window smashed, and blood was smeared over the broken glass that littered the seat. The engine was still running, but from the way it was sputtering, it didn't sound like it would be for long.

The cab had tumbled further down the embankment, barrelling through the gaps between the trees, and sometimes pushing them over with the force of its passage. It must have rolled at some point, because it was now lying on its roof in the leaf litter, but it took Kulika a moment to notice that. The first thing she noticed wasn't the car at all, it was the ring of zombies surrounding it.

How was it possible that there were so many of them? She'd come out here looking for three, but there must have been fifty times that number surrounding the car. The crowd was stacked five people deep in places, which begged the question: what exactly had Bartholomew been doing with the zombies his crew had created over the past six months? Bayly had told her they'd fed them to the gators, but the plentiful evidence standing in front of Kulika right now suggested that had been a lie. All these extra zombies had to be from previous failed attempts to make Silver. Where else could they have come from?

They didn't seem like normal zombies, though. None of them was making any attempt to move forwards. Instead, they were holding vigil at a distance of about ten feet from the car, leaving a perfect circle of empty space around the crashed vehicle. The zombies' feet were still, but everything else about them was in constant motion. They moved as a group, knees gently flexing and shoulders swaying in uncanny unison to give the eerie impression of waves rippling through the collective.

Kulika didn't stop to admire the effect, she just pushed her way through the zombies gathered at the closest edge of the ring. They parted for her like the Red Sea.

'Quick?' she called desperately, kneeling down beside the car. This close, she could see the blood spattered across the paintwork. There was a lot of it, enough that she started to panic.

But then a small voice whispered, 'Kulika?' from inside the car.

Kulika ducked her head to find Quick crouching in the front of the car, with Evita and Xiaoyu huddled in the back.

'Are you okay?' Kulika asked, scanning them all for any sign of serious injury.

They looked a bit bashed up, but beyond the odd scrape they'd all escaped the crash remarkably unharmed. Quick and Evita must have protected the human between them, because otherwise there was no way she would have survived a wreck that bad, not without a miracle.

But if they were all okay, why were they still huddling in the car?

'They must have followed us down here,' Quick whispered. Her fearful eyes were scanning the zombies behind Kulika.

'Then just shove them out of the way,' Kulika said, bewildered. 'They're just zombies. They won't hurt you.'

'But the sunshine will,' Quick said. 'I can't find my parasol.'

'And they'll definitely hurt me,' said Xiaoyu.

Then Quick dropped the bomb.

'They're contagious,' she said. 'One drop of their blood, and we'll lose Xiaoyu.'

7

IN THE MOMENTS following the crash, Quick was disorientated.

When the car had first shot off the road, she'd acted on instinct. She'd unclipped her belt as they careened down the embankment, then she'd forced her way into the back seat at speed as she'd felt the car start to roll, using the last reserves of blood in her body to get to Xiaoyu fast. Evita had the same idea, because she'd already wrapped herself around Xiaoyu, the only one amongst them who was likely to suffer permanent injury from a car crash. With the car flipping like it was, there was no way to get her out.

'Hold on!' Evita yelled.

Quick clung onto Evita, using their bodies to form a cage around Xiaoyu, then there had been an almighty crash. Everything went still.

When Quick blinked her vision clear of blood and smoke, they were all upside down. Unlike the others, Quick wasn't wearing a seatbelt, so when she relaxed her grip on Evita, she fell headfirst into the roof of the car. From her newly-prone position, she could see what the others couldn't: a little way up the embankment, the pick-up truck had stopped between two trees. The driver's side door was smeared with blood, and the glass in it had shattered. At first she thought the driver might have been thrown out of the side window, but then the door popped open and a middle-aged man stumbled unsteadily out. He was propping himself up on the body of the pick-up as he walked towards the cab, one hand trailing along the top of the door.

What happened next took only a fraction of a second. The man's hand slid into a tiny smear of blood on the top of the car door and then, as Quick watched in horror, he changed. First, he froze. Next, his eyes became bloodshot and he started crying bloody tears, as though the blood vessels had swollen and broken and were now streaming their contents down his face. Then there was the way he moved. When he'd first got out of the car, he'd been walking in a jerky, stumbling shuffle that suggested he was compensating for an injury. Now, his movements became rhythmic and fluid and horribly familiar.

All from touching one tiny drop of blood.

'Shit,' Quick muttered.

'We need to get out of here,' said Evita, working at her seatbelt. 'The petrol tank could blow.' Her belt sprung free and she joined Quick on the inverted roof, though she made the descent with more grace than Quick had managed herself. Then she started on Xiaoyu's belt.

'Mind the blood, Xiaoyu,' Quick said, slowly processing what she'd just seen. 'Don't even touch it.'

'But there's blood everywhere,' Evita said, stopping in the middle of ripping through Xiaoyu's seatbelt.

'Then don't touch anything.'

She quickly explained what she'd just seen happen to the pick-up truck driver, who was now standing in the trees just a short distance from their upturned car.

Evita gave her an incredulous look.

'I'm serious,' Quick said.

Evita's jacket was still stuck painfully to the raw skin on Quick's burned arm, wrapped around it in a mess of blood and pus. There was nothing Quick could do about that now. She'd only make it worse if she tried to remove it, but she wasn't healing either. She'd used the last of her reserves making sure Xiaoyu was safe from the crash. Thank god she hadn't infected her with any spatter in the process.

'And don't touch me, either,' Quick said. 'I can't tell how much of this blood is mine and how much came in through the window with the zombies.'

'Fuck,' said Xiaoyu.

'I'll move into the front,' Quick said, shifting along the roof in that direction. 'Then you'll have more space.'

It was awkward and claustrophobic, but Quick managed to wriggle out of the way and Evita got Xiaoyu down from her seat without too much trouble.

But the moment Xiaoyu hit the ground, everything went wrong again.

'Uh-oh,' she said quietly, looking out of the window.

Quick and Evita lay down to follow her gaze and saw that the pick-up truck driver was no longer alone. From their vantage point, Quick could only see up to their knees, but she was counting an awful lot of them, in every direction.

'Shit,' Evita muttered. 'Are they going to reach in here like they did on the road?'

'I don't know,' said Quick. She looked at the zombies again, but they weren't showing any signs of movement, they were just holding their positions in a ring around the car. 'The ones Bella turned in the garage acted like they were scared of us,' she said, trying to puzzle through it.

'That's not normal for zombies,' Xiaoyu commented.

'No, but they're not normal zombies,' said Quick.

'So,' said Evita. 'Options are: go out there or stay in here. If we go out there, Xiaoyu maybe turns into a zombie.'

'And I definitely catch on fire,' said Quick.

'But if we stay in here and the gas tank blows...' said Xiaoyu.

'Then the two of you go,' said Quick. 'Test it out first, Vee, to make sure they'll leave you alone. Then, if you've got enough energy for it, maybe you can run Xiaoyu out of here.'

'And leave you behind?' said Evita.

'That's the most slapdash plan I have ever heard,' said Xiaoyu. 'You're going to get me killed.'

'You got a better one?' Quick asked.

That's when they heard the voice outside. At first, Quick thought it was in her head, because surely she couldn't have conjured the one person she wanted to see more than anyone else in the world right now, but then the voice came again.

'Quick?' Kulika called. 'Are you in there?'

The zombies parted, a pair of black boots came into view, followed by a gloriously familiar face, with blonde hair falling into serious grey eyes. For the first time all morning, Quick felt like she could breathe again.

'Kulika,' she whispered.

Then Quick explained about the zombie contagion, and Kulika's face paled.

'From just a drop?' she asked.

'It looked that way from here.'

'Well, your car's fucked,' Kulika said, surveying the crumpled bonnet of the upside-down vehicle disdainfully. 'We'll have to take mine, but we're going to do this very carefully. Give me a minute to test it out.'

The zombies were still gathered thickly around the car,

though they'd stepped back a little from the spot where Kulika crouched. As she stood, they reared back further, and as she walked towards them, they parted like curtains to let her pass. When she came back the other way, they did the same, all while sticking as close to the car as Kulika's proximity would allow. They wouldn't get closer than about ten feet to Kulika, but neither would they give up on the potential prey that Xiaoyu represented. They were biding their time, waiting for their moment.

Calculating.

'You're right,' Xiaoyu said. 'Those are not normal zombies.'

'We can't leave them out here,' said Kulika. 'We're going to have to corral them back to the mansion.'

'With one working vehicle?' said Quick incredulously. 'Unless you have a lorry up there on the road, or one you can call, they're never going to fit.'

'They don't need to,' said Kulika, turning to Xiaoyu with a smile that made Quick worry. Rightly, as it turned out.

'We've got bait,' Kulika added.

Xiaoyu laughed and said, 'You're joking,' but she stopped abruptly when Kulika's expression didn't change.

She was deadly serious.

On the first run to the car, Kulika carried Xiaoyu while Evita trailed along behind, just in case. The horde of zombies followed. When Kulika returned a minute or so later without incident or escort, Quick started to believe this might actually work.

'They okay?' she asked.

'They'll be fine,' Kulika replied. She opened the driver's side door, crouched beside the upturned car and passed Quick a blanket. 'The zombies are surrounding the car, but they're keeping their distance while Evita's there.'

'Good.'

Which meant all Quick had to do now was engineer a sun shade for herself with one arm. The burn on the other was so severe she wasn't sure she could raise it at all.

'You're bleeding,' Kulika said, her brow furrowing as she spotted the bloodstained jacket wrapped around Quick's arm.

'Broken window,' she explained. 'I was driving. I caught on fire. You know, the usual.' She laughed, but the sound had a manic edge that gave her away.

'Can you manage the pain until we get back to the mansion?' Kulika asked, surveying her with concern. 'I've only got Bartholomew's tiny sports car, so you're going to be crammed in close, and I can't promise it'll be comfortable.'

She could manage the pain, right? It was just shooting, burning, prickling agony. And anyway, pain wasn't the real problem.

'I'm worried I got some of the zombies' blood on me,' Quick said. 'I don't want to transfer it to Xiaoyu. Our driver got pulled out through the window, and she turned, then I was up front, and...'

'Well, could you walk?' Kulika asked. 'If you keep alongside the car with the blanket held over your head like a parasol—'

'I'm not sure I can hold it up,' Quick admitted. 'With my burned arm, I mean.'

She couldn't bring herself to say aloud the thing she wanted most in that moment, so she tried to communicate it silently instead. Her eyes locked with Kulika's. For a brief flash, Quick could see the silver threading through the grey of Kulika's irises. Surely that meant she knew what Quick was asking for?

But Kulika didn't offer it. Instead, she said, 'I've got a bottle of blood in the car.'

'I don't want blood,' Quick whispered.

'I can't...' Kulika said, but her gaze flicked down to Quick's lips in a way that suggested she could be persuaded.

Kulika loved her, Quick reminded herself. That was what Evita had said. The proof of it was right there in her eyes, and that made Quick braver than she might have been otherwise. She reached one hand out, spreading her fingers over the padded ceiling of the car next to the spot where Kulika's own hand was resting. Then slowly, not wanting to scare her away, Quick moved her little finger until it was resting against Kulika's.

That tiny point of contact felt like an anchor. It pulled them together, clicking their bodies into place like magnets. With a sense of wonderful inevitability, Kulika was suddenly in the car beside her, her fingers sliding into Quick's hair, her lips just a breath away from Quick's own.

When the cool wave of Kulika's healing came this time, it came hard and fast, bursting across Quick's body from the spot where Kulika cradled the back of her head in her hand. So the silver mark would be hidden by her hair, Quick realised, but then there was no time for thinking. Kulika inhaled sharply, as though she was surfacing for air, and Quick found herself matching her breath without thinking. That was what undid her, finally. With that breath, Quick was surrounded by the fresh saltiness of Kulika's scent, like sunshine and sea air on bare skin, and she couldn't hold herself back any longer.

Thankfully, she didn't have to, because it was Kulika who closed the paper-thin gap between them. She kissed Quick hard and fiercely, as though she was searching for something she couldn't quite find. Quick was more than happy to let her keep looking a while, but she pulled away all too soon.

By that point, the two of them were sprawled across the

upturned ceiling in the front half of the car, lying in blood and broken glass and all the detritus that used to be on the floor and in the side pockets of the car: pens, coins, receipts, wires. It was tangling in Quick's hair and poking into her back, but she couldn't bring herself to care because there was Kulika lying half on top of her, the tips of her platinum hair tickling Quick's cheek, and one of her legs resting between Quick's. If she just bent her knee a little, she'd pull up the hem of Quick's dress with it and then maybe—

'You're healed,' Kulika said.

Quick looked down at her arm, from which Evita's jacket had now slipped free. Kulika was right: the skin was unmarked underneath the dried blood that covered it. By the time Quick looked up again, Kulika had slipped away from Quick like a retreating tide, leaving only cold emptiness in her wake. She was fully out of the car now, standing in the disturbed dirt outside the door. It had happened in a blink. Had she really just used Silver speed in her desperation to get away from Quick?

'Come on,' Kulika said, without crouching down to meet Quick's eye. 'We should get back to the others. Throw the blanket over your head and let's go.'

She didn't bend down to help Quick out of the car; she didn't even wait for her to follow, she just turned and started walking back up the embankment, leaving Quick to follow on behind with her makeshift parasol, as though nothing had just happened between them.

As though Quick's world hadn't just been turned upside down, with a crash and a kiss.

The flotilla that trundled along the road towards the mansion would have been a strange sight to anyone who had passed it, but thankfully this corner of South Carolina remained quiet. The only vehicle on the road was Bartholomew's little silver sports car, crawling along at snail's pace, surrounded by a fat doughnut of zombies. The blood covering the car's hood spoke to the time it had taken Kulika to adjust to the zombies' speed, but they were perfectly in sync now. The creatures ran constantly in that fluid, sinuous motion of theirs, backwards or sideways or forwards, whichever orientation allowed them to keep their eyes on the car, and on Xiaoyu.

In the passenger side, Xiaoyu was crammed together with Evita in the awkward bucket seat. Quick jogged alongside the car on the driver's side next to Kulika's open window, holding the blanket over her head. Kulika was keeping her close as a precaution, she had said, so she could get to Quick immediately if there was an accident and she started burning again. Quick was working hard to make sure that didn't happen for Evita's and Xiaoyu's sakes, though personally she would have suffered any number of burns to be kissed like that again.

'Why are there so many of them?' Quick asked, looking around at the zombies. 'Have they just been hunting along the highway?'

'No,' said Xiaoyu quietly. 'I recognise some of them.'

'There was a breach at the blood cellar,' Kulika confirmed. 'They got out. They must have run into the ones who escaped from the wine cellar and...' She looked around at the zombies who were running alongside the car. 'This is what happened.'

Quick made an involuntary noise somewhere between a sob and a sigh, choking on the enormity of it. Looking around at the horde that followed them, she thought she recognised a face or two as well. They were close enough for her see where the whites of their eyes should have been, but with the gore that now dripped and smeared across their cheeks, and with the distortions their changed states brought to their expressions and mannerisms, it was hard to be certain that they were familiar. It wasn't Quick they were watching, either; they were all looking at Xiaoyu, who seemed certain enough for both of them. She had her face pressed against the passenger window, her fingers spread wide against the glass. She had known most of these people personally, Quick realised. She'd lived with them, and kept them safe, and done her best to put herself between them and whatever creatures came down the cellar hatch to prey on them. If seeing them like this was upsetting for Quick, she couldn't imagine what it was doing to Xiaoyu, particularly since she was now their target.

'We can't turn them back to how they were, can we?' Xiaoyu asked.

'No,' said Kulika. 'They're gone. And anyway, look at them: with injuries like that, most of them wouldn't make it even if you could.'

Unwillingly, Quick's eyes were drawn to the zombies that circled the car. She started cataloguing their injuries: broken limbs, gored throats, stomachs that gaped open in a way that should have been fatal, yet left them still walking. When she started looking for the wounds that should have cut the zombies down, she couldn't stop seeing them. After that, Quick pulled the blanket down lower and kept her eyes on the road, trying not to look at all.

They'd been running for a mile or two when she noticed that something was up with Kulika. She watched her for a while, trying to work out if it was something to do with their kiss, but then she saw that Kulika was peeking over and around the zombies, trying to get a look at the tree line beyond them as she drove.

'What are you looking for?' Quick asked her.

'Nothing,' Kulika replied, but there was something off in her voice. Although her tone was blasé, it didn't feel convincing.

That put Quick on edge, and had her looking in the same direction for the next mile or so, scanning the trees. Then Evita noticed too, and she started doing the same. When Xiaoyu finally pulled her eyes away from her former cellar-mates for long enough to see what the others were doing, she got spooked.

'What's going on?' she asked.

Kulika sighed. 'I was trying not to worry you all.'

'I think we're already worried,' Evita pointed out. 'I can feel the anxiety coming off Quick in waves.'

'And I can feel it coming off you,' Quick said to Kulika.

'Really?' Kulika replied, as though that surprised her.

'Yes,' Quick replied. 'Really.'

Although Kulika wasn't showing anything on her face, which was as impassive and controlled as ever, there was a nervous energy to her that Quick couldn't see as much as she could feel it. Now that she was looking for the tell that had tipped her off, Quick couldn't pinpoint it, but nonetheless she knew in her gut that Kulika was worried.

'I still don't want to worry you all,' Kulika said.

'Tell us anyway,' Xiaoyu insisted.

Kulika hesitated for a moment, looking first around the ring of zombies that was keeping pace with the car, then from Quick to Xiaoyu and, finally, to Evita.

She said, 'The zombies aren't the only thing that escaped from the wine cellar.'

8

KULIKA'S STOMACH TURNED every time she remembered the look on Evita's face as she'd told them about Digs. She knew how traumatising her weeks spent alone in that box with him must have been. She'd been hoping she wouldn't have to say anything, but then Quick had noticed her looking, and she'd had to confess.

Kulika still couldn't understand how Quick had picked up on her anxiety. It wasn't as though Kulika went around broadcasting her emotions. She was a security expert with over three hundred years' experience and the kind of knowledge you couldn't get from training. When she was out in the field, she controlled her expressions, she controlled her reactions, and she controlled her respiration – such as it was – so there was nothing that should have tipped Quick off. Somehow, she'd just known.

Christ, she was dangerous. Kulika shouldn't have kissed her. And that look Quick was giving her now, as they drove the last excruciating half-mile up the road to the mansion? Kulika couldn't tell what that look meant.

In fact, she couldn't tell what Quick was feeling at all, which was strange. After a moment's confusion, Kulika realised she was missing something that had become so familiar she'd barely noticed it until it was gone: usually, she could read Quick's mood through the tone of her scent. Now, though, she was getting nothing. She could smell the complex mixed-seasons scent that was Quick's personal perfume, wafting through the car's open window, but it was no longer kaleidoscoping in the way that had become so familiar and intoxicating. It wasn't ebbing and flowing in the way it had done previously, which suggested there was something seriously wrong with Quick. Or maybe Quick's scent was behaving exactly as it always had, but Kulika could no longer perceive it.

She wasn't sure which of those possibilities was more terrifying.

Quick's scent wasn't the only thing about her that had gone awry, though. The red in her hair was somehow less bright, her perfume was generally less strong, and Kulika couldn't feel the air sizzling between them the way it had just last night, before she'd said her goodbyes. Maybe that was only because the others were in the car beside her, but surely their presence shouldn't be enough to stop the electricity jumping between Quick and Kulika as they crept along the road, mere feet away from each other? Being in company had never stopped that spark before. Besides, there had been the same strange absence in their kiss in the crashed cab, even though every look from Quick still had the same effect on Kulika as sunlight did on Quick's skin, starting rampant fires all over her body that she couldn't seem to quench.

Which left Kulika with one explanation: there was something wrong with Quick that her healing kiss hadn't been able to fix.

Kulika *really* shouldn't have kissed her. She'd known that

if she even touched her, Bartholomew's nose was sensitive enough that he would smell her scent on Kulika's skin the moment they got back to the mansion. Even the distance between them now was probably too close; tantalisingly, enticingly close. Quick was no longer hers, she reminded herself. She'd given up her claim, just as Bartholomew had given up his.

He'd make Kulika pay for crossing that line. She could only hope he wouldn't take her transgressions out on Quick. All she could do now was keep her distance, and try not to make the situation any worse.

Monty and a gang of the others were waiting in the driveway when they pulled up, gawping at the entourage she'd brought along with her.

Quick had moved to the other side of the car, wanting to be closer to Evita. That meant the ring of zombies bowed out wider on the passenger side of the car as they tried to avoid getting too close to Quick, so Kulika pulled up with the driver's side facing Monty and the other new Silver, keeping a fifteen feet gap between them and the outer edge of the ring; she didn't want to pincer the zombies' comfort zone and force them any closer to Xiaoyu.

'Round them up!' Kulika yelled at the crew. 'Come in slowly and corral them away from the car.'

'And be careful with them,' Quick added from the other side of the car. 'They're contagious.'

'What do you mean, *contagious*?' someone asked. With the ring of zombies standing between Kulika and the Silver, she wasn't sure who had spoken. Not that she would have recognised them anyway; she barely knew this crew she was supposed to be leading.

'I mean if any of them bites a human,' Quick said, 'they'll turn into a zombie.'

'Bullshit,' someone muttered. He was hiding in the crowd, but Kulika recognised the voice.

She slammed the driver's side door and stepped away from the car. The zombies parted theatrically to either side of her as she approached the gang of new Silver, giving her the kind of entrance that would have made Bartholomew proud.

'Got something to say, Monty?' Kulika said, getting up close to him, steely-voiced. 'Maybe you'd like to explain to me how all this happened on your watch in the first place?'

'*My* watch? I just look after the block.'

Kulika sighed loudly. 'And where exactly is the blood cellar?'

'Well…' Monty's initial reply was automatic, as though he couldn't help but argue. He couldn't follow it up, though. He, like the rest of the Silver gathered in front of her, had clearly been drinking.

Alcohol didn't usually have much of an effect on the Silver, but these ones were young and stupid, and had probably drunk far too much. No wonder they hadn't answered their phones when Penny called. No wonder they hadn't managed to find the zombies, either. Kulika was surprised they'd managed to find their own feet.

'Has anyone bothered to check the blood cellar?' Kulika asked. 'How did the humans get out in the first place? Is it secure enough to hold the zombies?'

'Yes,' Monty said. 'There's nothing wrong with it, it's just that the hatch was left open.'

Kulika had seen enough of that hatch to know it would be impossible to open it from the inside. That could only mean one thing: someone had opened it to let the humans out.

Kulika looked over the zombie horde to where Quick stood beside the car. She was holding the blanket too low over her face for Kulika to see her eyes. Maybe that was just a matter of perspective, since Kulika was no longer looking up at Quick from inside the car, or maybe Quick was hiding deliberately. Either way, Kulika had her suspicions about Quick's involvement in the escape. She hadn't made much of a secret of her desire to see the humans of the blood cellar liberated.

Hadn't Penny said there'd been a fire just before the escape? And hadn't Quick been caught just the night before, using a fire under the mansion's porch as a diversion so she could set the blood cellar free?

'Put them in the cellar,' Kulika said to Monty. 'And count them. If there's anyone missing, I need to know about it immediately. Assume the whole blood cellar turned, plus the zombies that were supposed to be locked up in the wine cellar. And there were two drivers they met on the road. I assume you know how many people were in the blood cellar to begin with?'

'Yes,' Monty replied, but he sounded worryingly uncertain.

'Then work it out,' she snapped. 'And we need people out on the highway looking for wrecks we might have missed. Where's Penny?'

'Here,' said a voice from the back of the crowd.

When Penny had pushed through the Silver to the front, Kulika grabbed her and pulled her alongside, so she was facing the others. 'Penny's heading up communications from here. You need to stay in touch with each other. If she calls you, you answer. Got it? I'm not having a repeat of this morning.'

'We've got to go silent when we're searching,' Monty argued.

'Then you make sure you're checking your messages regularly. Now get these zombies safely away.'

'What about them?' Monty asked, nodding his head at the car.

Quick and Evita were both outside now, guarding the passenger-side door from the zombie ring. Quick looked over at Monty from under her blanket and sneered, clearly unhappy to be returned to his company. Then she looked at Kulika. There was a question in her eyes, maybe even an offer.

But the answer had to be no. Quick couldn't stay here. None of them could stay. Kulika had made her bargain, and there was no backing out of it.

She had to let Quick go, again.

'Put them in the library,' Kulika said. 'As soon as all the zombies are accounted for, they're leaving. And they're not leaving alone.'

Dr Ross was sitting on a chair next to the bed in what had once been Bayly's room. The single was now full to bursting as Enzo lay there wrapped in Bayly's arms. They'd changed position slightly, so they were no longer as tightly coiled together as they had been in the bath, and what Kulika could see of Bayly's skin above the sheets looked to be in much better condition than it had been when she'd left. His finger had grown back, too.

'How are they?' Kulika asked.

'Getting there,' said Dr Ross, leaving the bedside to talk with Kulika out in the corridor. 'But we need more blood than I have.'

'I've still got this,' Kulika said, pulling the bottle out of her pocket. 'But I don't have any more to offer you.'

'It might not be enough,' the doctor said, taking the bottle sceptically, 'but I'll do what I can. You didn't find the humans?'

'No, we did.'

'Then where are they?'

'Back in the blood cellar.'

Dr Ross shook her head and said, 'I don't like using unwilling donors any more than you do, but in the circumstances—'

'The zombies are infectious,' Kulika said, then she explained what had happened out on the road. 'One bite, or one drop of blood, and they turn humans into creatures just like them.'

The doctor's eyes went wide.

'They all turned?' Dr Ross whispered.

'Yes. Quick saw it happen from just a tiny smear of blood on a car window. It was instant.'

'Oh my god,' the doctor muttered, leaning back against the corridor wall. 'The blood is contaminated,' she muttered. 'The woods are contaminated. This house is contaminated.'

Kulika thought about the pool of blood in the wine cellar, the blood on Bayly and Enzo's bodies, and all the blood on their clothes and shoes that they'd trailed up the stairs as they'd carried the two men to the bathroom.

'It'll be an epidemic,' Dr Ross whispered. 'Are there any other humans in this house?'

'There were human crew members when I first arrived, but I think they're gone now.'

'Good. That's good.'

Then a terrible thought occurred to Kulika: 'But the whole world is coming here this evening to watch Bartholomew launch his new ship.'

The launch party took a while to explain, as did the ship, but when Kulika had finished, the doctor looked haunted.

'You have to stop it,' she said. 'It'll be a bloodbath.'

'Bartholomew's never going to let the press into the house,' Kulika said. 'They'll all be down by the river.'

'And what if one of the escaped zombies went out that way before going into the woods? What if there's a drop of blood on the drive, or on the grass, or it gets on the bottom of someone's tyre or shoe, and they spread it even further? If it's as infectious as you say it is, then you can't take that risk, at least not until you've let me take a look at it under a microscope.'

Kulika groaned. This wasn't the news she wanted. She wanted to send the doctor home, and Quick along with her, as quickly as possible.

But after seeing what had happened out on the road this morning...

'Did you get your samples from the zombies downstairs?' Kulika asked.

The doctor patted her bag and said, 'I've got everything I need.'

'Then Bartholomew keeps the basics in his library. Everything's antique and outdated, but I've definitely seen a microscope on the shelves.'

'That'll do for now. Let me get this last bottle of blood into Bayly,' she said, hefting it in her hand, 'and then we'll see.'

'Please work fast.' Kulika took a deep breath and added, 'Because I need you to do me another favour too.'

The doctor looked at her quizzically.

'I need you to take Quick and her friend back to the UK with you.'

If anything, the confusion on Dr Ross's face intensified. 'I don't understand,' she said. 'I thought you love—'

'Which is why,' Kulika interrupted. 'I need you to keep her safe, please. And maybe just... keep an eye on her for me, okay?'

'What? Why?'

'I'm worried that there might be something wrong,' Kulika confided.

'With Quick?'

'She just seems different.'

The doctor's interest sharpened. 'Different how? Is it something to do with the zombies?'

'I don't know.' That was the fear Kulika was too scared to articulate. 'Her colours aren't as bright, and nor is her scent. And before you say anything, I know that makes no sense, but I'm telling you there's something off. I healed her earlier and it… I don't know. It didn't feel the same. With her sun sensitivity… I'm worried. You might want to take a look at her blood, while you're at it.'

Dr Ross looked at Kulika for a moment, assessing her. She said, 'Let me see your silver.'

'Excuse me?'

Amongst the Silver, a demand like that was not so much abrupt as it was downright rude.

'I said, let me see your silver,' the doctor repeated unrepentantly, leaning in close to Kulika's face. 'Something's off with you, so show me.'

'Nothing's *off* with—'

'Kulika,' Dr Ross said sternly.

'Oh, fine.'

Kulika relaxed the unconscious control she was exerting on her eyes, letting the silver flood back into the whites, and on into the irises. That extra reach – the silver in the grey of her eyes – was the mark of her bond to Quick.

Except it didn't feel right.

When she'd released control like this previously, she'd felt a gentle thud of satisfaction as the silver circled around her pupils, completing its course with a finality that settled reassuringly in her chest. This time, that didn't happen. She felt the silver reach, but she didn't feel it land. Something was off.

'What's happening?' Kulika asked.

'I can't… It's…'

The doctor leaned even closer, then reached out and pulled up one of Kulika's eyelids.

'Is it bad?' Kulika asked.

'I don't know what it is,' Dr Ross said, finally releasing Kulika and leaning thoughtfully back against the wall. 'I've never seen it before. It looks as though the silver is sort of… stuttering.'

'Stuttering?'

'Like it's being blocked, and only partially penetrating into your iris. It's not as though I've made an extensive study of this, you understand, because of course the sample pool is very small, and even if it wasn't, how could you experiment ethically? Of course, the Silver can heal from physical injury without too much inconvenience, but psychological injury? My days of manipulating the emotions of my subjects for the purposes of science are behind me, I can tell you that much for free.' The doctor laughed bitterly.

'Okay,' Kulika said uncertainly, not following.

'My point is,' the doctor said, re-boarding her train of thought, 'from a very cursory examination – *very* cursory – it looks as though the silvering is starting to reverse itself, which is, of course, impossible.'

'Reverse itself?'

'Exactly. And if the silver in your eyes is disappearing, that would mean—'

'The bond is disappearing too,' Kulika finished.

'Which is, again, impossible,' the doctor added.

But it would explain so much. The way Quick's touch suddenly left her cold, the distance she felt growing between them, the fact that Kulika could no longer discern Quick's mood from her scent. In fact, everything about Quick felt dulled to Kulika. The brightness of her hair, the variations in her scent, the electricity of her touch.

Oh, god.

The silvering was reversing.

'But why?' Kulika asked desperately.

'I don't know. Something must have changed.'

'Well, how do I stop it?'

'I don't know,' the doctor repeated hopelessly.

With a growl of frustration, Kulika turned and paced towards the stairs, leaning against the banisters as she looked down to the ground floor below. That was where it had all started, down in the hall on the night of the Casting. Was this how it was going to end, her silvering dissolving into nothing with a quiet sigh?

'Can I ask you something?' Dr Ross said after a moment.

'What?'

'Do you actually want to stop it?' she asked tentatively.

Kulika turned to face her. 'Of course I do. Quick's the only good thing in my life.'

'But she's not going to be in your life anymore. She's leaving again, and she's not coming back. Wouldn't it be easier if you could let the bond go with her?'

Maybe that was what had changed: Quick had left, and the bond was stretching thin with her absence. If she left for good, maybe it would stretch so thin that it became nothing at all. Would that be better than this pain in Kulika's chest, making her want to fold in on herself every time she remembered that Quick would never touch her again?

'Maybe,' Kulika agreed. 'If I had the choice, but it's not in my control, is it? Will you just look at her blood for me? Please?'

'All right,' the doctor agreed.

'Then the library's this way.'

Kulika started down the stairs, the doctor and her bag close on her heels.

'I don't suppose you found Digs?' Dr Ross asked.

'Not yet,' said Kulika. 'That's the next emergency on my list. Maybe ask me again in an hour.'

She led the doctor to the library, made brief introductions to Quick, Evita and Xiaoyu, then strode off outside to find Monty. She didn't want to hang around; she couldn't stand to look at the hope and expectation in Quick's eyes when she knew she was about to wipe it out. It was easier to deal with the task at hand, so that's exactly what she did.

She tracked Monty down to the block. He was hanging around the glass doors that led into the common room at the front of the building, watching the trees as though he was expecting someone to emerge from them any moment. When he saw Kulika coming, he stood up a little straighter.

'You got them all?' she asked him.

'I guess,' Monty said dismissively.

'No, not "I guess",' Kulika snapped back irritably. 'Do you understand what would happen if we left one of those things to wander around out there? So let's try again, shall we? Did you bother to count and make sure we've collected every single one of the incredibly contagious zombies you just allowed to be created?'

'Yes,' he said shamefacedly.

'The seven original from the wine cellar?' Kulika asked, still not trusting Monty's confirmation. 'And however many humans used to be in the blood cellar, and the driver—'

'I did a full count,' he said, finally acting like he was taking things seriously. 'I promise you, we've got them all. I'm sure.'

'Sure enough to swear it to Bartholomew?'

'By blood, if necessary.'

Which was just as well, because Kulika did not have time for this. She needed to check the zombies were secure, create a safe space for the press conference this evening, and find Digs, and she needed to do all of those things immediately.

'Where the hell is Bartholomew?'

'The Primus?' Monty asked, with an edge of disapproval in his tone.

So much for taking things seriously.

'Don't test my patience, kid.'

'He's still on the boat.'

'The *ship*,' Kulika corrected him. 'He was supposed to be back hours ago.'

As if on cue, Kulika saw the *Primus's Fortune* hove into view on the other side of the lawn, travelling upriver by virtue of a gentle breeze and a hell of a lot of manpower. A few of the crew who'd left with Bartholomew were down on the bank, heaving the ship along with the assistance of ropes and superhuman strength. Kulika dreaded to think how much blood they would have consumed to haul it against the current like that, for god knows how far. It was a lot of veins to open for the sake of a rich immortal's vanity project. Given the current drought, it might be the last they saw for some time.

'Sort your people out into search parties,' Kulika ordered Monty. 'Use runners for messages if you have to, but get them on a grid and be methodical. And keep half of them here to prepare for tonight. It's only a few hours until people are going to start arriving. We're running out of time. When I come back, I want to see this whole crew sober and organised.'

'Yes, Secundus,' he said.

Kulika couldn't tell if he was being mocking or obedient, but she also didn't care as long as he got the job done. Right now, she needed to speak to Bartholomew.

9

OF ALL THE people Kulika could have handed them off to, Quick thought Monty might have been the worst. He'd glared at Evita – who'd glared right back – grimaced at Xiaoyu, then looked at Quick as though she were a terrible disappointment.

'Stay here,' he'd told them as he'd bundled them into the library. 'And no snooping around.' Then he'd left and shut the door behind him. Quick heard the lock tumble.

She threw down the blanket, relieved to be rid of it, and looked at her two bedraggled friends.

'Idiot,' Evita muttered. 'He does know that I can bust right through that door, doesn't he?'

She slumped down into one of the library's armchairs and Xiaoyu took the other, leaving Quick with the chair behind the desk.

'I've decided I don't like being bait,' Xiaoyu said. Her voice was a monotone, her gaze hollow and haunted. After that long, torturous drive in the sun, she looked ten times worse than she had when she'd woken up that morning. 'I suppose I deserve it, though.'

'You don't deserve any of this,' Quick said.

'I was supposed to protect them.' Xiaoyu's face crumpled. If she hadn't been so dehydrated, she would have been crying. 'They were my responsibility,' she said, biting the words out through her grief. 'Them and so many others. It's my fault they're gone.'

'Hey, no.' Quick hurried back around the desk and perched awkwardly on the armchair, trying to take Xiaoyu into her arms. The other woman didn't want to be comforted, though. Her body was stiff and tense, shuddering with all the emotion she was trying to contain. 'This is not your fault.'

'I think I need to tell you both something,' said Evita. She was looking down into her lap and worrying at her cuticles; a nervous habit she'd had for as long as Quick had known her.

'About what?' Quick asked.

'Please don't hate me, okay?'

Quick scoffed. 'We're not going to hate—'

'Just hear me out.'

Then Quick registered the guilty look on Evita's face and realised she'd just made a promise she might not be able to keep. 'What did you do?'

'Before we left the mansion this morning,' Evita said, 'I did something potentially stupid.'

'Okay…'

'I was looking for Bartholomew,' she explained, talking faster now, like a penitent child, 'and I heard someone saying he'd been down in the wine cellar visiting Bayly.'

Quick groaned. 'You didn't. Please, Evita, tell me you didn't.'

'Seriously, hear me out. I just went down there looking for him, that's all. Can you blame me? Bayly and Bartholomew in one place… You think I wasn't going to speak my mind?'

'No,' Quick said on a sigh. No one had ever accused Evita of being a shrinking violet.

'But then I saw… something, and I ran, okay? I just ran. I think I left the door open.'

'Vee…'

'You don't understand.'

'What I don't understand is why you had to go looking for Bartholomew. We were nearly out of here.'

'I had to,' Evita said. 'Don't make me explain it. It was just something I had to do.'

'Well, you've certainly done it now,' said Quick.

If that sounded harsh, merciless even, then perhaps it was, but Evita had form for doing stupid things for stupid reasons.

Quick could be impulsive and impatient, yes, but Evita took it to another level. Like that time when they were undergraduates, and Evita had dosed herself with some kind of pill – to this day, Evita couldn't tell Quick what it had been, she'd just accepted the offer of a high from a vague acquaintance – started seeing colours, and hatched a brilliant plan to steal a keg from behind the student bar at five in the morning. Quick had intervened in time to save the keg from being accidentally rolled into the river, but not in time to stop them being caught by campus security. It was all on tape, of course. It was a minor miracle they hadn't both been kicked out, there and then, but Quick had spun a sob story and got them off with a harsh reprimand.

She'd thought those days were over, but apparently she'd been wrong. Now Evita hadn't just risked getting them both saddled with a criminal record, she'd started a zombie outbreak.

'Please don't give me that look,' Evita said. 'I didn't mean to let them out, if I in fact did, which I maintain is debatable. It was an accident.'

'It was careless.'

'And you're perfect all the time, are you?'

'No, of course not! But I didn't start a fucking zombie apocalypse, either.'

'It's been averted, all right?'

'After people died, Vee. Our driver. The guy in the truck. All those people in the blood cellar. All dead.'

'I know,' Evita said, chastened. 'And I feel terrible, but I didn't know they were contagious. I thought they were just regular zombies, except for the fact that they don't die.'

'It wasn't you,' Xiaoyu said quietly. 'It was me.'

'What?' asked Quick. Xiaoyu had been quiet for so long that Quick had started to forget she was there at all.

'It was me who killed all those people,' Xiaoyu said again. 'It's my fault they're dead. I was the one who started the fire and opened the blood cellar.'

'What?' said Quick. 'No, Xiaoyu, that was me. Last night. I started the fire at the back of the mansion then got you out of the blood cellar.'

'Which is where I got the idea, but no,' she insisted, her voice a haunting monotone. 'When you were both sitting on the doorstep this morning, and all the other vampires were busy partying, I went back to the block, opened the blood cellar hatch – fairly simple with the right leverage – then set a fire on the other side of the building as a distraction while everyone got out. I didn't know there were zombies in the woods, or that they were contagious, but when I say this is my fault, I mean it. It's my fault they got turned into… whatever they are.'

'You were just trying to help,' Evita said.

'And I still got them all killed,' Xiaoyu replied.

'I should have done the same,' said Quick. 'You weren't to know that—'

'Stop,' Xiaoyu said. 'Just… stop. I know what I did. Let me make peace with it.' Then she turned away, staring out of the window and into her own thoughts.

She was clearly done talking.

Quick closed her mouth around the placations she was about to spout. There was no point; Xiaoyu had sunk so far down into her misery that there would be no pulling her out of it. She'd have to swim through it on her own.

When Quick turned away from Xiaoyu, she found Evita glaring at her. She would have asked what the problem was, but then the key turned in the lock to the library door, interrupting whatever pseudo-sibling bust-up they were about to have.

In the second before the door swung open, Quick could smell the sea, only Kulika's scent was *better* than the sea. It was fresh and light and charged with sunshine and hope. Just one breath of it was enough to set Quick's heart racing before Kulika had even stepped into the room. She was open-mouthed and expectant, rising from her perch on the edge of Xiaoyu's chair as her hopes rose with her.

Only to be dashed the moment Kulika walked inside.

'Dr Ross,' she said, avoiding Quick's eyes. 'These are Patience Quick, Evita Khalyed and Xiaoyu…' She paused, apparently waiting for Xiaoyu to fill in the blank with her surname, but Xiaoyu just carried on staring out of the window. 'Xiaoyu,' she finished. 'Microscope's somewhere on the shelf up top. Help yourself.'

Then she left, closing the door behind her without speaking a single word to Quick.

Kulika had kissed her, just this morning. She'd held her in her arms, and healed her burns, and made her feel like she wasn't the only one whose skin was on fire.

But now: nothing.

Nothing at all.

'Nice to meet you all,' said Dr Ross with a smile. She was

a short, round woman with a cheerful face and a strong Scottish accent. Her hair was messy and her lab coat was stained, but she had an air of openness and competence that Quick found instantly appealing. 'I've just got a few tests to run, then we'll be on our way to the airport. Ms Quick, I'll be needing a sample of your blood, if you don't mind obliging me.'

'Why?'

'Just a control sample,' the doctor said, then she dragged the desk chair up against the nearest wall and started poking around on the top shelf of the bookcase. 'Take this, would you?' she asked Quick, handing down an ancient-looking microscope and a couple of boxes. 'On the desk, please.'

Once she'd poked around on the shelf to her satisfaction and found nothing else she wanted, Dr Ross hopped down to the ground and carried the chair back around the table, then she opened the bag she'd brought with her and started pulling things out.

'I need a clear workspace, please,' she said as she set up the microscope and started peering down it, examining slide after slide. 'If all of you could stay on that side of the room, it'd probably be for the best. These are dangerous chemicals. Especially for you, Ms Xiaoyu.'

Xiaoyu ignored her entirely, still staring out of the window. Quick looked over at Evita, wondering what her reaction was to the whirlwind of Dr Ross, but Evita turned away and looked out of the window with Xiaoyu.

Sulking.

Quick wasn't the only one who noticed.

'What's up with you lot?' Dr Ross asked, looking up from her slides.

'Nothing,' Quick replied.

'Just tell her,' Evita muttered from her armchair.

'Fine.' Quick sighed. 'Xiaoyu's the one who let the people out of the blood cellar, and Evita's the one who left the wine cellar open.'

'By accident,' Evita hissed at Quick.

'By accident,' Quick agreed. 'But yeah. She let the zombies out.'

'No, she didn't,' Dr Ross said, putting her eye back to the microscope.

Quick was nonplussed for a moment, then she insisted, 'Yes, she did.'

'I really did,' Evita added.

'Maybe you left the door open,' said Dr Ross, looking up at Evita, 'but you didn't let the zombies out. They'd already got themselves free on their own. They tunnelled out through the floor, following Digs.'

The sigh of relief Evita let out was so large it must have been filling her whole chest. 'Did you find him?' she asked.

'Oh, I'm not looking. I'm the doctor, not the search party. I'll see him right when he's found, but until then I've got other things to bother about. Now,' she said to Quick, 'about that blood sample?'

10

'PHINCHAS!' KULIKA YELLED, striding to the dock where he was standing beside the *Primus's Fortune*. 'Wolfrie!'

The two men grabbed her around the back of the neck and pulled her close, the three of them pressing their foreheads together to seal their reunion. For the first time in more than a hundred years, Kulika was breathing the same air as them, inhaling the smoky fireside scent of Wolfrie and the sawdust scent of Phinchas. Together, the two of them smelled like camping on the beach and falling asleep in a tumbled heap of rum and stolen silks.

They were here.

They were *really* here.

They were deceitful, violent bastards, but they were *crew*, and she could trust them to get the job done. Their mere presence settled the anxiety roiling in Kulika's stomach.

Phinchas was a tall, lanky man with brown skin and watchful eyes. Wolfrie was the polar opposite: shorter, bearded, barrel-chested and gruff. Neither of them was the kind of person who would come across to a stranger as warm, but then Kulika herself was not warm either.

Bartholomew's crew had always been known for their spikes rather than their softness.

'When did you arrive?' she asked, pulling back to assess them both. Perhaps unsurprisingly, they looked exactly the same as they had the day she'd left. The clothes had changed – jeans and T-shirts now instead of breeches and shirts – but otherwise they were the same old Phinchas and Wolfrie.

'Just now,' Wolfrie said. 'Came up on the new *Fortune*.'

'You mean the *Primus's Fortune*,' Phinchas corrected him. Wolfrie scoffed.

'Insubordination, Wolfs,' Phinchas chided. 'And in front of the Secundus, no less. Would you have me beat him, sir?' he added to Kulika.

'Just tone it down in front of Bartholomew, will you?' Kulika asked quietly. 'He doesn't have much of a sense of humour these days.'

'Did he ever?' Wolfrie asked with a laugh.

'I'm serious,' Kulika said. 'Right now, I don't have much of one, either.'

She explained about the zombies, about the wine cellar, about Digs, Bayly and the hole in the wine cellar floor.

'That wily bastard,' Wolfrie said.

'He's not Digs anymore,' Kulika warned him. 'Not like you might remember him.'

'You never knew him in the first place,' Phinchas pointed out.

'No,' Kulika agreed, 'but I'm guessing he used to be more than a mouth and a set of teeth. Just watch yourselves, okay? You'll want to check in with the kid, Monty. The one in the green T-shirt.' Kulika pointed off towards the block, where Monty was organising the younger crew members into groups out on the lawn. 'Work out where he's searched, and where he hasn't. I've told him to organise the others, but make sure he actually does, okay?'

'Unreliable?' Wolfrie asked.

'Inexperienced,' Kulika said. 'And can you get some of the better noses searching around this area?' she asked, indicating the space on the riverbank where a stage was in the process of being constructed. 'The driveway, too. We need to know if any of the zombies came out this way, and if they did, every trace of them needs to be cleaned away by eight thirty. Ceremony starts at nine.'

'You got it,' Phinchas said. 'We'll pull some of the crew off the ship to help.'

'What do you think of her, then?' Wolfrie asked, patting the bow of the *Primus's Fortune* affectionately.

'She's a replica of the ship Bartholomew died on,' Kulika muttered. 'It's… creepy.'

'Pretended to die on,' Phinchas corrected her.

But it hadn't felt pretend to her. Bartholomew had made her promise, as he'd prepared for the final sea battle with the *Swallow*, that she'd find his body and throw it overboard before the British could capture it. He would heal, he'd told her. It was the only way for him to get them off his back, he'd told her. She'd known all of that, of course, but there was a strange madness to knowing something to be true while seeing evidence with your own eyes that directly contradicted that truth.

Bartholomew *had* been dead that day. His body had fallen on the main deck, close to the cabin door, his throat so riddled with grapeshot that his head was barely attached to his shoulders anymore. And the blood.

So much blood. Bartholomew's blood, that she shared.

It had felt sacred to her, back then. In those early days, he had been Kulika's god. To take his broken body in her arms and throw it over the side of the ship for the sharks that circled in the Gulf of Guinea…

He'd found her in new Port Royal, a week later, alive and well and exactly as he had always been. Kulika had never been able to erase that image from her mind, though: the lolling head, the shredded flesh, the disrespectful *smack* as his body had flopped onto the water below the ship. She remembered it as clearly as she remembered his second false death, a hundred years later, at her own hand: surprise on his face, the power she'd felt as his heart beat between her fingertips, the visceral force it took to break open his ribs with her bare hands.

With that much behind them, how could there be a future for Kulika on Bartholomew's crew?

'Hmm,' Wolfrie murmured, dragging her back to the present.

He and Phinchas had concerningly contemplative looks on their faces.

'What's wrong?' Kulika asked. 'Why are you both looking at me like that?'

Phinchas and Wolfrie looked at each other, then Wolfrie said, 'We heard you silvered.' He was looking at her eyes, as though he would be able to spot the silver she was masking just by squinting really hard.

'I don't want to talk about it,' Kulika said, striding towards the rope ladder that stretched from the deck of the *Primus's Fortune* to the dock below.

'It's nothing to be ashamed about,' Phinchas pointed out.

'Well,' Wolfrie said, 'it might be considered a weakness. I heard the girl is new.'

'I heard the captain was jealous,' Phinchas added.

'I heard he turned a girl himself,' said Wolfrie.

'I heard that, too.'

'I heard the captain *fancied* the girl he turned,' Wolfrie

added. 'The new one, I mean. Obviously, he's not pining after his Secundus, here.'

They both laughed, and Kulika's patience began to wear thin. She turned with her foot on the bottom rung of the ladder. 'And who exactly is telling you all this when you only just arrived?'

Wolfrie shrugged. 'People tell us things,' he said.

'We're likeable guys,' Phinchas added.

'You're manipulative bastards, is what you are,' said Kulika.

Wolfrie shook his head. 'All I'm saying is: has anyone seen Bartholomew's silver lately?'

Kulika thought back over the past week, but no, Bartholomew had never flashed his silver at her. That didn't mean anything, though. It wasn't something the Silver generally did, because it was more than just a gesture. When you revealed your silver to someone, you were inviting them in, or offering a threat. You didn't do it lightly. Unless, of course, like Quick and the other newbies, you were too young to hide it at all.

'I'm not sure he's capable of love,' Kulika said uncertainly.

'Maybe not what you'd call love, but...' Wolfrie shrugged. 'I heard the captain kissed her. That kid you pointed out, Monty? Saw it all, I heard.'

'No,' Phinchas said incredulously.

'Yes,' Wolfrie insisted.

The worst thing was, Kulika believed it. It occurred to her that she'd never spoken to Monty while she'd been conducting her first interviews with the crew into Evita's whereabouts. Monty had brought all the other new Silver to her, but he'd never volunteered any information himself, even though she knew he'd been here from the very beginning, like Evita. He was probably the only other person in the world who knew what had happened between Bartholomew and Evita, and he had kept his mouth firmly shut.

With Kulika, at least.

'I'm serious,' Wolfrie went on. 'Think about it: the captain turned her Silver, and he hasn't done that ever, for anyone.'

'Except Kulika,' Phinchas interjected.

'Right,' Wolfrie agreed, 'but she was a special case. This Evita… Well, imagine the possibilities. If he really has silvered for her, then we could take him out, once and for all.'

'By killing Evita?' Kulika said, horrified.

Wolfrie shrugged again. 'Small sacrifices.'

Small sacrifices.

That had become their motto at the mansion in the old days. Giving up piracy to hide their true nature? *Small sacrifices.* Putting one crew member down to keep peace amongst the others? *Small sacrifices.* Abandoning your crew to Bartholomew's whims because you couldn't hold yourself together a moment longer? Well, maybe that sacrifice hadn't been quite so small. It wouldn't have felt that way to Phinchas and Wolfrie when she'd left, Kulika was certain.

But the way they were talking now…

'Bartholomew is your Primus,' said Kulika forcefully. The rest of her patience had evaporated, along with her good mood. 'It doesn't matter whether he's silvered or not, or who he's silvered for, because that information is never going to cross your lips again. I mean, Christ, Wolfrie. Did you come back here just to start a mutiny?'

'No,' he said, blinking in surprise. 'We came back for you.'

'But you're sworn to him,' she pointed out.

'No,' said Phinchas. 'We're not. Not anymore. We bought our way out years ago. When Wolfrie says we came back for you, he means it. We came back for *you*. To get you out.'

Kulika shook her head, unwilling even to admit that idea into her mind. She couldn't leave. She could never leave. She'd bought Quick's freedom with her own, and the consequences of breaking that deal were too terrible to contemplate.

'You may not be sworn to Bartholomew,' she said hopelessly. 'But I am. We have a covenant,' she added, showing them the black spot on her palm.

They hadn't known. She could tell that easily enough from the way their faces fell.

'If you really came back for me,' she said, 'then I need you to do what I've asked you to do. So are you going to fall in line with me, and with the Primus, or am I going to have to find someone else who will?'

'Nope,' Wolfrie said, holding his hands up in surrender.

'We're already gone!' Phinchas called.

And they were indeed gone, disappearing into the trees at speed, searching for Digs: the man they'd called their crewmate before Kulika had even been born. Perhaps they should have had more loyalty to him than they did to Kulika, but reversals in favour were common fare for pirates. No one's word or friendship meant much for long, not without the enforcement of blood or threat.

She could only hope that Wolfrie and Phinchas's loyalty would last for long enough to get them all out of this mess.

11

QUICK AND EVITA were bored in the library while Dr Ross carried on her work in the kitchen – better light, she said – so they were indulging in their default activity: bickering. Xiaoyu had fallen asleep in her armchair, so at least they had some privacy.

'You're pining,' Evita said. 'It's revolting.'

'She didn't even look at me.'

'Because she's busy. Would you rather she dealt with the zombies or soothed your ego?'

'It's not ego! You said she was in love with me.'

'Right, so why are you being so pathetic about this? *She* loves *you*, not the other way around.'

'And how do you know I don't love her? Maybe I do.'

'Because you're not the one with silver in your irises, are you? Did you not listen to a word I told you in the car?'

'Well, I'm sorry I neglected to retain every detail of a conversation we had just moments before we were attacked by zombies. Clearly that's a sign of some great moral failing on my part.'

'No, the moral failing is that you actually want a vampire to have feelings for you.'

'So you're only dating humans from now on, are you? How do you expect that to work out for you, now that we're both vampires?'

'Better than your relationship with Kulika is, clearly.'

On and on it went, relentlessly. It sounded almost like normal banter, but it had too much edge for their usual back and forth, particularly when it should have been tempered by their recent reunion. They were both raw, and suffering, and they were rubbing up against each other's sharp edges. Quick could just accept that as part of the process of resettling their friendship, and maybe she should, but she couldn't let it lie. She wasn't destined to live up to her first name.

'Why are you sniping at me?' Quick asked abruptly. 'What did I do?'

Evita crossed her arms and pouted. For a moment, Quick thought she wasn't going to spill the beans, but then she uncrossed her arms and turned back with a fierce look on her face that Quick recognised. It meant she should run for cover.

'You're so ready to forgive Xiaoyu,' Evita said, 'but you come down on me for a mistake that it turns out I didn't even make?'

'Because Xiaoyu was trying to do something good. She was trying to save people. You were just chasing Bartholomew around the mansion like some kind of avenging angel! And now Digs is loose, and god knows what he'll do.'

'I do,' Evita said quietly.

'Do what?'

'I *know*. I spent weeks locked away in a box,' Evita said quietly, 'with him.'

Quick could feel her cheeks cooling as the colour drained

from them. She hadn't known.

'With *Digs*?' she said.

'With Digs,' Evita confirmed. 'I haven't forgotten how dangerous he is. I lived it every hour of every day for weeks and weeks.'

'Vee,' Quick said in horror. 'Why didn't you tell me?'

'What did you expect me to say? You want me to relive it for you, in every gory detail?'

'No! Of course not. But I didn't know.'

She also hadn't asked, though. She'd got the impression that Evita hadn't wanted to talk about her time in the box, so she'd left it alone. She was now realising belatedly that this was a story she should have asked for herself, rather than waiting for Evita to volunteer it. In her defence, it had been a hell of a day, but her neglect made her feel like a crappy friend, as did the bickering.

She slumped into the desk chair Dr Ross had recently vacated, all the fight going out of her. The moment she stopped resisting, Evita did too, relaxing back into her armchair with an exhausted sigh. They were both stretched so thin that it had been inevitable that they would break, sooner or later, but it was time Quick stopped making things worse for her friend.

'I'm sorry,' she said.

'Yeah.' Evita's reply was neither an acceptance nor a rejection. It was evasive instead, which hurt Quick more. She and Evita had never kept things from one another. Not before the mansion.

'I didn't think about what it must have been like for you,' Quick said. 'I'm sorry, Vee. I'm really sorry. Did you want to talk about it, or…'

Evita chewed on her bottom lip, avoiding eye contact. At first, Quick thought Evita was just going to ignore her, but then she said, 'You know the first thing I saw when I opened the door to that wine cellar?'

'Tell me,' Quick said, dragging the chair over so she could sit beside Evita's armchair.

'I saw this stuff smeared on the brickwork, thick and black like tar. But I'd seen it before. I'd spent weeks with it sticking against my bare skin, so I knew what it was and what it smelled like, and I ran. I was too scared to do anything else.' Evita's eyes were so wide that Quick could see white all the way around her irises, and her lips were trembling as she spoke. 'Maybe Digs didn't get out that way, but he could've done. I was too scared to stop. I didn't think about the door being open or what else might have been down in the cellar with him, I just saw that smear of black shit and I ran.'

Evita curled in on herself as she pulled her knees towards her chin.

'But you're right,' she said quietly. 'I shouldn't have gone looking for Bartholomew in the first place.'

Well, now Quick felt wretched. What was she supposed to say to that? The trauma Quick had gone through herself in the blood cellar, and at the Casting, and at the block... All that was nothing compared with the weeks Evita had spent locked in a box with a monster.

And the months before that? In truth, Quick had no clue what her friend's life had been like at the mansion before Bayly had cut it short by literally burying her alive.

Quick shuddered.

'No,' she said quietly. 'I'm sorry. I know Bartholomew deserves to suffer for what he's done—'

'Do you actually *know* what he's done?' Evita asked, her expression sharpening.

Quick laughed bitterly. 'Where do you want me to start?

He's responsible for all of this, isn't he?' She gestured around the library, but she was really encompassing herself, Evita, Xiaoyu, the whole property, and every broken person in it.

'Yes,' Evita agreed, but then she added, 'and no. None of this was here in the beginning, you know. It was just me, and Monty, and... *him*.'

'Just the three of you?' Quick asked.

Evita nodded, just a little, then looked down at her hands as though she had nothing more to say. If she'd wanted to leave it there, Quick would have accepted that, but it didn't feel like she was done talking.

'What happened to bring you here, Vee?' Quick asked, more softly now. 'Last thing I heard you were going to do your talk for the Charleston Pirate Association, and then you were gone.'

Evita took a deep breath, then let it out again slowly. After that, it all came tumbling out.

'Bartholomew came to the talk,' Evita said, sounding as tired as Quick felt. 'We spoke for a bit. He was rude and condescending... Well, you've met him. Afterwards, I went to that seafood place Richard Lewis is always banging on about. You know, the one with the fit barman?'

'Oh god,' said Quick, remembering her own path to this place. 'The one where Monty works.'

'You found it too, then?' Evita laughed darkly. 'I thought that might be how you ended up here. We always did have the same terrible taste in men.'

'That little shit really has no business being that good looking.'

'Funny how it wears off when you get to know him.'

'And how fast,' Quick agreed.

'He wasn't the one who brought me here, though,' said

Evita.

'No?'

'No. That was Bartholomew.'

Quick's stomach sank. If she thought she'd got herself in over her head in her association with Kulika, she couldn't imagine what it must have felt like to find yourself the target of Bartholomew's attention.

'He came to the bar,' Evita said. 'I kept telling him to leave me alone, but he wouldn't take no for an answer and… Fuck. Look, I thought he was hot, so maybe I wasn't *really* telling him to leave me alone. Maybe I just wanted to see how hard he was willing to fight for me. It sounds so stupid now, but when he looked at me in that predatory way that made every instinct in my body twang and tell me to run away, it twanged other things too. Hard.'

'Oh, Vee.'

'I'm not proud of it, all right? But I wasn't intending to act on it either. I swear, I was on the verge of turning and walking away, but then he told me all my theories about pirates reinventing themselves were correct. He said he could prove it. He told me he could show me the Articles of Agreement of Bartolomeu Português and his fellow buccaneers, the holy grail of pirate history. And then he actually did it.'

'They were real?' Quick breathed.

'Oh, they're real,' Evita said. 'And he should know; he bloody wrote them. They're probably in this room somewhere,' she added, looking around at the shelves of books and glass-fronted cases. 'Along with god knows how many other relics that could prove my theories. For all that it matters now.'

'But… Bartolomeu Português?' Quick asked. She didn't know much about Evita's field of study, but she knew enough to know the name of the buccaneer who'd founded the pirate code.

'Bartolomeu Português, Bartolemé de las Casas, Bartholomew Sharp, Bartholomew Roberts,' Evita said. 'He was all of them, and probably more besides.'

'Then you were right,' Quick said, feeling a little overawed. 'The old buccaneers really were reinventing themselves under new names.'

'I was right, and now I can't tell a soul about it. Can you imagine how I'd explain it?'

'Pretty easily after Bartholomew's revelation this evening. You can go back to the university in triumph.'

'Ha,' Evita said without humour. 'Some triumph.'

Kulika had filled them in on the launch party as they'd driven back to the mansion earlier. Quick has assumed they'd be gone again in time to miss it, but the afternoon was already rolling into evening, and here they still were.

'You know we're never leaving this place, right?' Evita said quietly. 'Bartholomew doesn't just let people go.'

'But he did let us go,' Quick argued. 'We just had a little setback. We'll be on our way soon enough. You'll see.' She tried to sound convincing for Evita, despite her own concerns.

'If the doctor isn't back in an hour, I want you to promise me we'll just take a car and go,' Evita said quietly.

'But she's got her own plane,' Quick pointed out. 'She can take us straight back to the UK.'

'If Bartholomew doesn't stop her first. Please, Quick, don't give him time to reconsider. He only wanted me gone because I remembered what he did.'

'What *did* he do?'

Evita paused for a moment, shifting in her chair. 'I told you I was at the bar with Bartholomew and Monty,' she said.

'Yes?'

'I woke up in his bed.'

'Monty's?' Quick asked, knowing that wasn't the *he* Evita meant, but hoping to hell that it might be, because the alternative was too terrifying to contemplate.

Evita tutted irritably. 'You know Monty never turned anyone before the girl last week.'

'Angelina,' Quick supplied.

'Whatever. My point is: no, Monty didn't turn me.'

'But you're saying that Bar—' Quick interrupted herself to lower her voice, just in case. 'You're saying *Bartholomew* did?'

'He bit me,' Evita confirmed.

'But Kulika said she was the only person he'd ever turned.'

'Well, maybe she was, until me. Or maybe he's been turning people for years and just never told her. I don't know, but what I can tell you is the last thing I remember before I woke up in his bed was his teeth in my neck. Of course, I didn't remember that at the time. When I woke up, it was like my whole life had been washed away by his blood. I remember it now, though.' The anger burned in her eyes. 'I remember it *all*.'

Quick couldn't parse her friend's emotions. She was angry, yes, but there was more to it than that. There was pain in her eyes, but grief too, and something else that Quick couldn't believe.

'What aren't you telling me?' she asked.

Evita fiddled with her cuticles, pushing them back and picking at the edges, avoiding the question. Finally, she stilled.

'He didn't just bite me,' she said, looking away from Quick as she whispered the words. 'He kissed me first. And

'I...'

Quick's mouth had dropped open, but she closed it again to ask, 'You what?'

Evita swallowed. 'I wanted him to.' She turned to Quick with a pleading look in her eyes. 'I kissed him back.'

12

KULIKA BURST INTO the cabin of the *Primus's Fortune* without knocking.

Along the back wall, where late afternoon light streamed through the windows set into the ship's stern, there was a desk and matching chair. The desk looked a lot like the one that Bartholomew had in the library back at the mansion, the desk that had once resided in the cabin of his flagship. In fact, it was so alike that Kulika had to stop to confirm to herself that they were not one and the same – but no, this piece of furniture was new, unmarred by the blade marks, candle burns and bloodstains that scarred the original.

It was the same story with all the furniture in the cabin: a map table she recognised from the parlour, chairs that strongly resembled the ones in the mansion's breakfast room, and a bed in one corner of the cabin that was the spitting image of the one that Bartholomew slept in today. It was more than that, though: these weren't just reproductions of Bartholomew's things, they were reproductions of the things he'd had back on the *Royal Fortune* three hundred years ago. Walking into the cabin was like stepping back in time, and it chilled Kulika to her bones.

Mostly.

Almost every part of her wanted to close her eyes and block out the memory of the terrible things they'd done in this room, but the part that was speaking the loudest wanted to revel in the rebirth of the venue of her crimes. She had been powerful in this place once, or in a place that looked a lot like it. Returning here sent the same power rushing through her again. It was a warm welcome from the side of her she had tried to forget, but that had not forgotten her.

Bartholomew should have been used to to Kulika's abrupt entrances by now, but apparently he hadn't been expecting her, because she caught him leaning against the bed frame, staring at a playing card that had Evita Khalyed's face on it.

'Regretting our bargain?' Kulika asked.

'Of course not,' Bartholomew replied, slipping the card into the back pocket of his jeans. 'Sending that woman away was the best thing I could have done, for all of us.'

'Right,' Kulika murmured, pointlessly delaying the inevitable. 'About that...'

'If you're about to tell me that—' Bartholomew stilled mid-sentence, his expression frozen on his face while a single nostril twitched.

Shit.

'We had a blood bargain,' he snapped, his lip curling upwards to show his teeth. 'Given its terms, perhaps you'd like to explain to me why you reek of Patience Quick?'

He pushed off from the bed frame and strode across the cabin towards her, grabbing her by the neck and pinning her against the opposite wall. If he wanted an answer from her, Kulika wasn't sure how he expected her to give him one while he was crushing her larynx.

'I can smell her on your skin,' he whispered, leaning in. 'Her odour has sunk into you like rot sinks into meat. I can smell her on your fingers.' He ran his nose along her cheek and sniffed. 'I can smell her on your lips,' he growled. 'I can smell her on your breath.'

'I had to heal her,' Kulika gasped, scrabbling at his hand with both of hers, trying to pry it away from her neck. 'The zombies infected the humans from the blood cellar. They attacked Quick's car. I had to bring them all back here to lure the zombies back. Quick got burned.'

'Badly enough to threaten her life?' Bartholomew asked, his grip as tight as ever. 'Badly enough to threaten *your* life?'

He saw the answer in her eyes. As his grip squeezed tighter, she didn't have the breath to speak it.

'You gave me your word that you wouldn't touch her again,' he said. 'You broke it.'

He dropped Kulika to the ground, then turned his back on her and started walking away.

'And you broke your word,' Kulika croaked from the floor, rubbing her throat. 'You gave me your word that they'd be out of here this morning.'

'And they were!' Bartholomew yelled back, uncontrolled in a way Kulika had rarely seen him. 'I promised you they'd be off the property, and they were. If you hadn't brought them back—'

'You would have preferred I left them in a ditch to get torn to pieces by whatever the hell these new zombies are?'

'Them, or their pet human?' Bartholomew countered scathingly. 'Even these new zombies can't kill the Silver.'

'But Digs could. Did you know that he got loose, and that he ate half of Bayly on his way out? Dr Ross thinks he's been contaminated by the zombies you locked up in the wine cellar with him. He's not interested in human blood anymore. He wants *ours*.'

Bartholomew practically growled in frustration. 'We wouldn't even be in this mess if you hadn't insisted on bringing Drake's little doctor here with her Silver-killing, zombie-horde-making formula.'

'And I wouldn't have needed to do that if you hadn't turned Evita Khalyed Silver.'

'And you think I don't regret that every single day?' he yelled. 'I don't need you to tell me that was a mistake because believe me, I fucking know.'

Shoulders heaving with his ragged breath, Bartholomew put his hands on the desk with his back to Kulika and hung his head. She pushed herself up to her feet, keeping her back against the wall and her eyes on him. She hadn't seen him this angry since the night she'd left him the first time. It made him unpredictable, so Kulika paid attention.

'I would see you rid of this bond,' he muttered finally.

Kulika laughed bitterly. 'It's the only reason I signed your covenant. Without it, you wouldn't have me at all.'

'But I don't have you now, do I?' he asked. 'Your head is somewhere else, at the beck and call of a Silver so new she can barely use her powers, performing petty healings when you should be walking into glory at my side.'

'You have my contract in blood,' she said, taking a tentative step forward.

'And you still broke it.'

'Not intentionally. She's not staying, Bartholomew. None of them are staying. I'm packing them off with Dr Ross and sending them to the airport, just as soon as the doctor's had a look at the blood of the new zombies.'

Bartholomew really did growl this time.

'We need her expertise,' Kulika argued. 'With Enzo… indisposed' – another growl – 'she's the only person in South Carolina who can tell us what we're dealing with. We need to know what threat the zombies present, and how we can get rid of them safely. I've already gathered them all up. Now we just need to clear the premises for tonight's launch party.'

The set of Bartholomew's shoulders softened, and she knew she had him. There was a smile in his voice when he said, 'I heard you went fishing for zombies with the pet human.'

'Oh?'

'The kid called.'

And hadn't said a word to her about it, the little creep. Kulika would have to deal with him, sooner or later. She supposed she should be grateful he hadn't blabbed to Bartholomew about Quick and Evita from the start, for all the good that delay had done her.

'I also heard what you did to my car,' Bartholomew added.

'Honestly,' she said, 'the zombie came out of nowhere.'

'Hmm,' he grunted, which made it clear just how irritated he was. She had to turn away to hide the petty grin on her face, which is when she noticed the room's focal point.

'Why is there a painting of me on the wall?' she asked, horrified to see her features rendered in oil and hung in a massive gold frame above the bed in the captain's cabin. The pose was dramatic: one of her feet rested on the prow of the ship while she balanced on the rail with the other, her long hair blowing back in the wind as she faced into a thunderstorm. The artist had made her look like some kind of Valkyrie, rather than the bloodthirsty demon she had truly been three centuries previously.

'It's a reproduction,' Bartholomew said dismissively. He stepped to her side to admire it with her, though for Kulika "admire" was definitely the wrong word.

'A reproduction of *what*?'

'Of the painting that hangs in the mansion.'

Then she remembered what Evita had told her when Kulika had first rescued her from the coffin on Bayly's boat: *There's a painting of you in his bedroom.*

'Why do you have a painting of me in your bedroom?'

'Because you belong at my side,' he murmured. 'I knew you would leave me. I planned against that eventuality, but weapons as sharp as you only become blunted when you keep them sheathed. You needed to use your claws. Of course, I would have preferred you hadn't used them to rip out my heart and run away with that bastard Drake, but… Still. I wanted a way to keep you close to me until you returned.'

'You were so sure I would?'

'You are the only person in the world on whom I can rely.' He turned to face her so they were chest to chest instead of shoulder to shoulder, and too close. 'I have always been sure of you.'

'And Evita?'

He flinched. He tried to control his reaction, but his eyes tightened a fraction, his head jerked back the tiniest distance, and irritation hitched up the side of his lip before he could tamp it down.

'The girl should be long gone,' he said.

'But it bothers you that she isn't?'

He shrugged, pretending nonchalance. Kulika wished she could do the same. She shouldn't care what Bartholomew felt for Evita. It shouldn't matter that he had turned her Silver, or that Kulika was no longer the only one who carried his blood. She couldn't understand the crushing sensation she was feeling in her chest, but she couldn't deny it either.

She was riling at the competition.

'What is she to you, Bartholomew? Really?'

'What are either of them, to us?' he whispered, reaching out to cup Kulika's face in his hand. 'New and soft, without any understanding of the lives we live now and have lived before. You and me, Kulika? We're sharp, like blades whetted against each other. No one can ever be to me what you are, nor be to you what I am. Without you, this endeavour has no meaning. I can't be Primus without you at my side.'

Without thought, Kulika felt herself leaning in to his touch, rubbing her cheek along his palm as a cat might rub at the ankles of its owner. The gesture was entirely involuntary. It brought with it a shudder of pleasure she hadn't been looking for, and had never expected to find at Bartholomew's hand. Here was the electricity she'd been searching for in Quick's touch, but had failed to find. Here was the thudding *rightness* she had missed. It was backwards, and beyond her comprehension, but it was undeniable. With Bartholomew's skin pressed against hers, she felt a connection.

She belonged with him. She belonged *to* him.

He'd been right, all those days ago: without him, she was an empty thing.

'What do we do now?' she asked quietly.

'We send them away, as though this morning never happened, and we send Drake's spying doctor away with them.'

'But the zombies—'

'You've contained them, and we can get more humans.' He laughed. 'They'll come to us. This evening, everything will come good. You'll see.'

'But Digs—'

'Is a minor inconvenience,' he said, stroking her cheek

and soothing her soul at the same time. 'You'll find him. Relax. You've done well, my Secundus.' He brushed the hair back from her face, letting his fingers rasp gently along the shaved portion of her head.

The sensation tugged at a memory of someone else, but Kulika couldn't recall why. Then a flash of scent surfaced in her mind – blackberries, frost, earth – and the name rose to her lips without conscious thought.

'Quick,' she breathed.

Bartholomew's face darkened for a moment, then he smiled and said, 'Come, sit.'

Bartholomew led Kulika to a chair, then circled the desk to sit behind it, opening the desk drawer. The runners rumbled ominously with the weight of its contents. When he pulled out the book, it fell open immediately to a page coated with dense writing in Kulika's hand – and blood. She wondered about that. How many hours out of the past twelve had he spent poring over those words, creasing the spine, revelling in his final possession of her?

The thought should have made her angry, but instead she felt a whisper of satisfaction at being so desired. It thrummed in her veins and thudded to the slow rhythm of her heart. He wanted her to belong to him, and that made her worthy of possessing. If she was not possessed by him, she was worth nothing at all.

'Shall we do this again?' he asked softly. Then he pulled the metal-tipped quill from between the pages of the book and offered it to Kulika by the feather end.

'What do you want me to write?' she asked, confused.

'Nothing,' Bartholomew replied. 'I don't want you to write anything. It's all here already,' he added, running his palm across the page. As he did so, tiny particles of blood released their scent into the air: copper and decay,

Bartholomew and Kulika, wound together like a braid and bound with ocean spray.

Bartholomew didn't explain any further. Instead, he took a second quill from the top drawer of the desk and used it to slice a bloody line down the centre of his palm.

The sight of it shouldn't have made Kulika thrill the way she did. The sensation was so foreign that she didn't even acknowledge it at first, but then her mouth began to water as the scent of Bartholomew's blood reached her nose, and she could no longer hide her hunger.

The scent was like nothing else. It wasn't salt, or sugar, or copper, or spice. Instead, his blood smelled somehow of life itself. It was everything.

Last night, it hadn't called to her like this. Last night, they had exchanged blood by pressing their bleeding palms together, but now it didn't feel like that would be enough. Kulika wanted more than just the passive flow of blood from one vein to another. She wanted to take it and fill herself with it. She wanted to bite it out of him, and taste him on her tongue.

Her gaze drifted from his cut palm to the vein at his neck, drawn there without her consciously willing it.

Bartholomew followed her gaze.

'Oh,' he said, a soft smile twitching at his lips. 'So that's how you want to do this?'

He stood from his chair and tossed it out of the way, paying it no mind as it clattered to the floor, then circled the desk towards Kulika.

'Take it,' he said, offering her his palm.

She didn't hesitate. She was salivating, her thirsty tongue already reaching out to lap at his hand as she grasped it to her mouth. She closed her eyes and groaned, then he groaned, and for a moment she forgot who he was supposed to be to her. All she knew was his blood, and how much she thirsted for it. Then the wound healed itself – he had always been a fast healer – and Kulika was left with nothing but a dry mouth and a hunger she couldn't sate.

She moaned her frustration, gripping his hand more tightly as the well ran dry.

'You want it,' Bartholomew said, closing his hand around hers to pull her to her feet. 'So take it.'

As she rose, she opened her eyes to see what he was offering. There was the copper token he wore at his throat, pulled to one side. There was his long, dark hair, cascading over one shoulder as he inclined his head. There was his henley, tugged open with one hand to bare his neck.

He was *baring* his *neck*.

Bartholomew Roberts didn't bare his neck for anyone. He'd certainly never done it for Kulika in all the long years of their acquaintance. The offer was shocking enough that she could do little more than stare.

'You don't need your meat cut for you,' he whispered into her ear. 'You have teeth.'

That was all the invitation she needed. Before the thought even reached her brain, she was biting into his neck and moaning again, this time with the pleasure of her conquest.

'My feral little pirate,' he groaned. Kulika felt the vibration through her teeth. 'Whatever am I going to do with you?'

Anything, Kulika wanted to say, but her mouth was full of his blood and she couldn't spare the time to speak. She wanted to consume him, to take little pieces of him inside her and let them breed in her bones until she was filled with nothing but him. When his teeth pierced her neck, sending his saliva deep into skin and muscle and vein, she thrilled to it. What had felt like violation only days before now felt like catharsis.

She needed this. She needed him to rinse away every trace of the person who had been in her arms before and replace them with himself. She wanted to forget, and she could forget three hundred years if she gave herself over to him. It could be the Golden Age again. He could be nothing but a pirate king and she could be nothing but his weapon, wielded and directed by his hand. She would surrender to him if it meant that she'd no longer have to feel the pain of all the love she would never have.

He wanted her, and that would be enough.

When he finally drew his teeth from her neck, Kulika forced herself to do the same. The dissatisfied noise she made when doing so was not intentional.

'I always knew you would come back to me,' he whispered, cupping her face in his palm. 'My Kulika.'

There was a quiet gasp from the other side of the room. Kulika turned quickly, attuning her hearing to pick out the nearest heartbeats, and beyond Bartholomew's she found another, human. It belonged to a pair of eyes that was peeking out from underneath the bed.

'You've got a stowaway,' she said, hastily wiping the blood from her mouth with the back of her hand.

'Oh, yes,' Bartholomew said. 'I'd forgotten about him.'

'Who is he?'

'Just a human from the historical society who thought I hadn't noticed him creeping onto my ship when we stopped at the harbour. He can wait.'

Bartholomew took Kulika's hand in his and licked the blood from it, watching her eyes for her reaction every step of the way.

She didn't pull back. She should have done, because not only did they have an audience, but they were fast nudging up against a line that the two of them were not meant to cross. Despite that, she found herself enjoying the feeling of his mouth on her skin. It was an abrupt change, but perhaps – like the reversal of her silvering – it was one she was meant to embrace.

There was a scuttling sound from the other side of the room.

'Impatient, Aloysius,' Bartholomew said with irritation, then he dropped Kulika's hand and raced at Silver speed to the other side of the room. He caught the human before he'd managed to get out from under the bed, then he pinned him down onto the mattress with a foot resting across his neck.

'You're Kulika,' the human said reverently, his gaze flicking in disbelief between the painting on the wall above his head and the real deal standing in front of him. 'And you're… you're…'

'You know my name,' Bartholomew said. 'We've been working on this ship for long enough.'

'But you're *the* Bartholomew Roberts. You're over three hundred years old.'

'Five hundred, actually, but who's counting?'

'And you,' the man breathed, his eyes lighting up as he looked at Kulika once more. 'You are the living embodiment of all I ever dreamed.'

Kulika didn't like the sound of that.

'Steady on,' she said.

'I told them,' Aloysius said triumphantly. 'I found the sketches from that very portrait, and I read the stories about the capture of the *Onslow*, and I *told* them that you fell in love with her and dressed her up as a pirate so you could take her to sea with you.'

'Excuse me?' Kulika said. She'd been following him for the first part of his speech, but then it had taken a sharp left turn into the land of what-the-fuckery.

'Dressed her up?' said Bartholomew. 'I assure you, Aloysius, she was not *dressing up*.'

'And he isn't in love with me,' Kulika said.

The human laughed. 'I've been in the room this whole time,' he said. 'He was *licking* you.'

Shudders raced down Kulika's spine, but she couldn't tell whether she was creeped out or... something else. Bartholomew had always had that uncanny edge to him, the hunger in his eyes that made you ride the boundary between fear and attraction, but Kulika couldn't remember ever having come so close to tipping over it before. Worse, she couldn't bring herself to care that she almost had.

'Shall I get rid of him?' she asked Bartholomew.

Bartholomew laughed. 'Still thirsty, my little pirate?'

'Still security-conscious,' she countered, 'in light of this evening.'

'Oh, I don't think Aloysius will be any threat to our event,' Bartholomew replied, eyeing the grey-haired human with consideration. 'In fact, now that our blood cellar has run dry, I think he might be exactly what we need to prove our point,' he added, then he touched the tip of his tongue to one of his canine teeth.

Kulika heard Aloysius's gulp.

Bartholomew just grinned and grinned.

13

IN THE MANSION'S library, Quick was growing itchy. Part of this could be ascribed to her general impatience, but most of her restlessness had been building as Evita had sat hollow-eyed, telling her story after story of the deaths and deviancies she'd experienced during her time at the block. Now that she'd started talking about it, she didn't seem able to stop, the horrors pouring through her teeth in bitten whispers and gasps. After hearing all that, Quick could finally appreciate how much worse it was for Evita to be back here than it was for Quick herself.

'I'm calling a cab,' she said, pulling the doctor's phone out of her bag. Evita was right: they shouldn't be here, and they needed to go.

'Without the doctor?'

'Like you said, she's got her own plane. She can leave in her own time.'

Quick held the phone up, getting no reception at all, then looked around the library for a landline, in vain.

'Shit,' she said. 'Look, you get your stuff together. I'm going to go outside to get a signal.'

'Not on your own,' Evita said, standing from her chair.

'With Digs on the loose—'

'Well, we can't leave Xiaoyu here, can we?' Quick replied, gesturing at their sleeping friend. 'Just… I'll be right back, okay? Just be ready.'

Evita gave Quick a warning look that told her she'd bloody well better be right back, then Quick slipped out of the door – Dr Ross had left it unlocked, bless her – and into the halls beyond.

It was quiet.

Quick's every step creaked and clacked on the floorboards in a way that made her certain someone was going to come running to lock her back in the library where she belonged, but they didn't. In fact, she made it all the way to the porch before she saw another soul at all.

Then she saw *her*.

Kulika was striding along the side of the pool with her head down, barrelling towards the porch door like a woman on a mission. It reminded Quick of the first night they'd met, when she'd watched Kulika striding towards a conversation with Bartholomew like she was striding into battle. God, she was incredible.

Then she looked up and saw Quick, and paused mid-step.

Quick wanted to imagine that Kulika had frozen for the same reason she herself had: because the sight of the other woman made it difficult to catch a breath. When Quick met Kulika's eyes, she didn't just see flint-grey threaded with silver, she saw a world of possibilities that spread out in front of her like the wide horizon over the open sea.

But Kulika's eyes were turning stormy now, her silver hidden once more. She looked angry.

'You were supposed to wait in the library,' she said, brushing past Quick without looking her in the eye.

'I was trying to get reception to call a cab,' said Quick,

following Kulika inside the mansion. 'What happened to your neck?' she added, her eyes drawn to the wound at Kulika's throat. It was healing – nearly healed, in fact – but she could see broken skin and indentations in her flesh. 'Is that... did someone bite you?'

'No,' Kulika said, running her hand over the wound. By the time she removed it, there was nothing there at all.

'Was it Digs? The thing that was in the box with Vee?' Quick asked. 'Did you find it?'

'*Him*,' Kulika corrected her. 'And no.'

A terrible feeling began to churn in the pit of Quick's stomach. She remembered the night that Kulika had turned her Silver, and all that had entailed. She remembered the unexpected ecstasy of Kulika's bite and the way it had blazed through her body in an unstoppable wave. The feeling surging through her now was an entirely different kind of fire.

'Someone bit you, though, didn't they?' she said angrily, following close on Kulika's heels. She had no right to be jealous, but she couldn't help it. Kulika had healed her – kissed her – just hours before, and now she had someone else's teeth marks in her neck.

Kulika abruptly turned around, and Quick nearly barrelled straight into her. They were close, so close, for a tantalising moment, then Kulika stepped back, putting space between them that Quick wished she could obliterate.

'I'm sorry,' Kulika said, her voice cold and distant. 'For what happened back at the car... I shouldn't have done that. You should leave, now.'

'I'm not leaving until you give me an answer.'

It was the wrong thing to say. Quick knew that the moment the words had come out of her mouth, but she couldn't call them back. They were out there now, casting more storm clouds through the grey of Kulika's eyes.

'I don't owe you that,' she said, her voice terrifyingly calm. 'I don't owe you anything.'

'I know,' Quick said desperately. 'I know that, and I know I don't have any right to ask for an explanation, but I need one. Look, Vee told me you've silvered for me, because otherwise you wouldn't be able to heal me, and that it means you must have feelings…'

Kulika looked away, biting her lip irritably. She clearly didn't want to have this conversation, but Quick wouldn't be able to live with herself if she didn't ask.

'Please,' she said. 'I just want to know what all this means.'

'It doesn't matter what it means,' Kulika said. 'You need to go, and I need to stay.'

There was lead in Kulika's words.

'You could come with me,' Quick said. 'You don't want to be here any more than I do, do you? We could run together.'

'From Bartholomew?' Kulika laughed incredulously, as though it were inconceivable.

'From everything,' Quick insisted. 'From Bartholomew, from this plan of his, from his country. Why not? We could just be us, somewhere else.'

Kulika didn't show any outward reaction that Quick could see, but all the same she could feel Kulika's wanting. It was hot and tight, filling the space between them with an intensity that Quick didn't understand, and was afraid to ask about.

'And what if I don't want to run from him?' Kulika asked.

It wasn't until then that Quick realised how badly she'd misread the situation. She went cold, then hot, then itchy with embarrassment.

'You're barely a week old,' Kulika said. 'Bartholomew

has lived for half a millennium. He made me to be his equal in ways that you could never be mine. What makes you think that I would *ever* give him up for you?'

There should have been words spoken, then. Quick should have been able to find them, on the tip of her tongue, in her pockets, or pulled up from the earth through the soles of her feet. There were none, though. Her heart was empty, her hands were empty, her mouth was empty.

There were no words. She just stood there and hurt.

'Go home, Quick,' Kulika said as she turned and walked on to the library without a backward glance. 'There's nothing for you here.'

For a moment, Quick couldn't move. Her temperature was all wrong, and she could feel her pulse in her tongue. Was she going to be sick? She felt like she was going to be sick. Actually, she felt like she'd just been punched in the stomach by an articulated truck. She wanted to curl up in a ball and cradle herself until it stopped hurting, but something told her that wouldn't help, not here. Instead, she stared at the floor until she got her breath under control, wiped away the tears she hadn't noticed she was shedding, and shakily followed Kulika back to the library.

Where she found Xiaoyu still asleep in her chair, but Evita nowhere to be seen. Quick was certain that the windows had all been closed when she'd left the room a few minutes ago, but now the one behind the desk was open.

No, not open, missing entirely. There was glass on the floor. Glass, together with smears of a sticky black substance, somewhere between treacle and tar.

'No,' Quick murmured, racing to the window. There was blood on the couple of shards of glass that still held in the frame, but nothing beyond except a few trampled plants in the flowerbed outside. 'No!' she yelled out of the window.

'Evita!'

Not again.

She couldn't lose her best friend again. They'd barely begun patching up the rifts that had been punched through their relationship by the trauma they'd each suffered in this hellish place. It couldn't end here, with two broken girls, who'd become broken women, fracturing apart at the hands of an irrevocably broken man.

'Don't touch the blood,' Kulika said, all business. 'Get over there,' she ordered, 'next to the human.'

'You mean Xiaoyu,' Quick corrected her, not quite believing the change that had come over Kulika since this morning.

'Just go,' Kulika snapped.

Quick was used to seeing warmth in Kulika's eyes, sometimes humour, and even a painful edge of longing that Quick was all too familiar with herself. She still felt that longing when she looked at Kulika, but it was no longer reflected back at her.

Now, there was nothing in Kulika's eyes at all.

'You want me to go?' Quick asked. 'Fine. I will.'

Then she grabbed her blanket, leapt through the window, and ran. At superhuman speed, frantically burning through the last of the energy in her exhausted body. Now that Quick had finally begun to understand the pain Evita had suffered at Digs's hands, there was no way she was going to leave her to suffer again alone. She could see a faint trail of blood and black ichor, and she followed it haphazardly across the lawn towards the river.

Haphazardly, because it was possible that she'd slightly miscalculated the protection she'd get from the tattered old blanket she was holding above her head. There were new rips in it that she was sure hadn't been there earlier. When she'd been walking down the road under it this morning, she'd had a little protection from the trees, too, and the sun had been overhead. Now, the dying light shone sideways across the open lawn from the horizon, cutting right under her cover and slicing into her face like a hot blade.

She could hold the blanket low enough to protect her skin, or she could hold it high enough that she could see where she was running to, but she couldn't do both, however hard she tried.

'Quick!' Kulika yelled, already close behind. 'Stop!'

Her arms were burning. Her face was burning. There was a noise like a kettle boiling and Quick realised that she was screaming through her gritted teeth as she ran, but she kept following the spotty black trail nonetheless. She followed it all the way across the lawn, through the trees, down to the river, where it split in five directions, each apparently as fresh as the other. One went right down to the water, another past a dock where an incongruously large ship was moored, a third back through the trees at a slightly different angle, the fourth across the lawn to the block, and the final one along the riverbank. Dozens of Silver were moving at speed in that area, putting the finishing touches to a bank of seating and a little stage in front of the dock.

Quick had no idea which direction was the right one to follow.

'Fuck!' she yelled.

The Silver working on the stage turned to stare.

'Did you see anyone come this way?' she called over to them.

'Besides a woman literally on fire?' Angelina called back.

Quick shifted the blanket, wrapping it around her forearm to quench the flames that were starting to crackle along her skin, but in the process she managed to dislodge the whole thing, and now her face was burning too. It wouldn't be long before her eyes melted shut—

The pain.

God, she'd forgotten it could get so bad.

Then something hit her in the side and tackled her to the ground, rolling her onto the dock and into the shade of the ship.

'You have to stop,' Kulika said desperately, looming over her, holding her shoulders down against the cool wood of the dock, as though she thought Quick was intending to go right out into the sun again. 'Please. I'm sorry I was… Just stop.'

'They came this way,' Quick said, struggling gingerly up onto her elbows. 'They came this far, at least, but then the trail goes off in all different directions—'

'I know, and we'll follow it. But you have to go back inside.'

'I can't just leave her,' Quick said, salt tears scalding their way through the raw skin on her cheeks. 'Not again.'

'And you won't have to. Look,' Kulika said, pointing to the trees in the west, 'the sun's already setting. In fifteen minutes, it'll be dark, and if my team haven't already found her by then, we'll go out searching together. But you can't do it like this.'

'I have to—'

'Quick,' Kulika whispered. 'For the next quarter of an hour, please, just let me handle it.'

There was more softness in Kulika's eyes as she spoke than Quick had seen all afternoon. Quick was no longer certain if that meant something, or nothing at all, but she couldn't argue with the sense of Kulika's words.

Quick was no use to Evita like this.

'All right,' she agreed hopelessly. 'I'll wait.'

Kulika's gaze softened further, so much that Quick

wondered if she was about to take back everything she'd said in the house. All Quick could see was silver-grey eyes and a face she wanted to wake up next to every day for the rest of her life, but what was Kulika looking at? Quick wished she knew. The silver in her eyes should mean that Kulika loved her, but with everything that she'd said earlier today…

Quick just wished she could trust her.

There was a sound like a fist slamming into a wall, loud and startling, and the dock shook beneath Quick's back. Kulika abruptly pulled away. Bartholomew had jumped from the ship, and now he was standing behind Kulika, looking down at them both with an expression of angry disapproval.

Kulika didn't turn to face him immediately. Instead, she closed her eyes for a moment, then hissed at Quick, 'Sit in the shade. Don't say a word.' After that, she stood and turned her back to Quick, putting herself between Quick and Bartholomew.

'Primus,' she said.

'Kulika,' he replied. 'You told me you were sending her away.'

'And I am, as soon as possible, but Digs has taken Evita.'

For a moment, Quick thought Bartholomew looked almost concerned. His brow pinched, just for a fraction of a second, one that Quick probably wouldn't have noticed before she'd turned Silver, but all traces of that concern were immediately replaced with rage.

'Then find him, find her and deal with it!' he yelled. 'Have you forgotten that the press are arriving within the hour?'

'No, Primus,' Kulika replied. 'I'll see it done. I just need to heal Quick's wounds, then—'

'Oh, no,' he interrupted. 'I don't think so. I think she

needs to feel the consequences of her actions for once. Don't you?'

Quick looked down at the raw red of her arms, felt the burning in her cheeks, and began to regret her choices.

'She goes back to the mansion,' Bartholomew said. 'You go out on your hunt. And kill him, this time, will you?'

'Kill him?' Kulika asked.

'Yes,' Bartholomew confirmed. 'Kill him. Dead. I've got everything I wanted from him.'

Then Bartholomew returned to the ship, leaving Quick to wonder what, exactly, he had wanted from the monster that Digs had become.

'Back here again?' Xiaoyu asked Quick when Kulika deposited her back in the library.

'Back here again,' Quick agreed, defeated. 'You know what happened?'

'I can guess,' Xiaoyu said. 'It's not good, is it?'

'Digs took Evita,' Kulika said, then she took a key out of her pocket and used it to unlock a high cupboard on the wall behind the library door. It swung open to reveal a handful of old guns that looked like they belonged in a museum. Kulika stuck two fingers in her mouth and whistled out of the library door, so loudly and at such a pitch that Quick had to cover her ears.

'What are you going to do?' Quick asked Kulika, but she didn't get an answer before a couple of strangers joined them in the library.

'What the hell were you doing?' Kulika was yelling at the two men. 'How did he come back to the property and get into the mansion – into the *library* – when you were supposed to be tracking him?'

The tall, skinny one said, 'We did track him. We tracked him round and round in circles. He's crossing over his trail, trying to throw us off, so we can't work out where it starts or finishes. Whatever he's turned into, his brain's still working just fine.'

'And his teeth are, too,' the other man said. He was the polar opposite of the first, short and round and covered in hair. 'We found two dead Silver in the woods.'

'Not Evita?' Quick said desperately, snapping the men's attention to the corner of the room where she and Xiaoyu were standing.

'Two young men,' the hairy one clarified, and Quick nearly collapsed with relief.

Meanwhile, the tall man had frozen, staring off over Quick's shoulder.

'Xiaoyu,' he breathed.

Quick looked at him, then at Xiaoyu, then back again. Xiaoyu did not look pleased.

'Um, Xiaoyu?' she asked.

'Quick,' she said stonily, 'meet Phinchas. The lying shit who abandoned me here six months ago.'

Excellent, Quick thought. *More drama. Perfect timing.*

'I can't believe you're still here,' he whispered to her.

'Why?' Xiaoyu replied defiantly. 'Did you expect me to be dead by now, drained dry in that fucking blood cellar?'

'The… What?'

'Oh, come on. Don't even try to pretend that you didn't know what was happening when you dumped me here with *him*.'

'Who, Bartholomew?' Phinchas said, wide-eyed and innocent-looking. 'He said he'd look after you.'

But Xiaoyu wasn't buying his act. 'Go fuck yourself.'

'Later,' Kulika said, fiddling with the guns she'd retrieved from Bartholomew's safe. They were old, and rusty, and Quick was certain they weren't going to be enough to take down Digs. 'Phinchas. Wolfrie. You said you couldn't find Digs because you couldn't work out where the trail started? Well, you have his starting point now, so go. It stops down at the dock, then splits five ways. Follow them all. I'll be coming after you in ten minutes.'

'Yes, Secundus,' Wolfrie said with a lazy salute, then they went, with Phinchas looking mournfully behind him the whole way.

'I'm going to find the doctor. Xiaoyu,' Kulika said, 'look after Quick.'

Quick was confused by that for a moment, until she turned to see Xiaoyu rolling up her sleeve to bare her wrist.

'Hey, no,' Quick said, backing away. 'I'm not taking her blood. She's still an invalid.'

Kulika made a *tsk* noise and said, 'One sip won't kill her, but it will heal you. If you want to come looking for Evita, you'll drink.'

'You told Bartholomew I'd stay at the mansion.'

'I know what I told him,' Kulika said irritably, then she left the room, leaving Quick and Xiaoyu alone.

'Let me,' Xiaoyu insisted. 'It's the only way I can be useful.'

So Quick let her. It was fast – just a tiny puncture to her vein with the point of the knife that served as Bartholomew's letter opener – but effective. The puncture had practically closed by the time Quick had drunk her mouthful, along with the burns on Quick's exposed skin.

'Thank you,' Quick said.

'Don't thank me,' Xiaoyu said bitterly. She had been crying. There were no tears on her face, or on her sleeves, but Quick could see their ghosts in the redness that still coloured her eyes. 'I'm sorry,' Xiaoyu said, looking out of the broken window towards the river. 'I shouldn't have fallen asleep.'

'It's not your fault,' Quick replied, her voice as hollow as she felt. 'I shouldn't have left the room. I was trying to get phone reception to call us a cab and finally get us out of here, and then—'

'I didn't even wake up,' Xiaoyu said, shaking her head. Then she stopped, frozen, looking out of the window. 'Is that a ship at the bottom of the garden?'

'Yes,' Quick said, tossing the phone back into the doctor's bag before joining Xiaoyu at the window. 'A frigate, I think. Pirate ship.'

'You know a lot about it?'

'Evita does,' Quick said quietly.

Evita would love that ship, Quick thought. She'd had ship diagrams taped all around her office back at the university. She'd always been talking about how pirates would capture navy vessels, then convert them with more cannon, and bigger cabins to accommodate the whole crew, not just the officers. No elitism on a pirate ship, she'd said. Pure democracy.

Well, that hadn't been Quick's experience of being on Bartholomew's crew. That hadn't been her experience *at all*.

'We'll get her back,' Quick said.

'We'll get her back,' Xiaoyu repeated, taking Quick's hand in her own. 'Then we'll get in that car, and we'll drive to the airport, and you'll fly away. I'll get back to my kids, and everything will be okay.'

'Do you really think that?' Quick asked.

'No,' Xiaoyu admitted. 'But isn't it nice to pretend?'

14

KULIKA FELT LIKE weeping. She didn't actually weep – she was holding vicelike control over her emotions, crushing them down at the slightest hint of rebellion – but she felt like doing it all the same.

The *burning*. She could still smell it, coating the insides of her nostrils. The raw wounds on Quick's cheeks and arms had not been as bad as the first time she'd burned, so Kulika was reassured that her tolerance to the sun was slowly increasing, but she was worried by how slowly the wounds were healing. There just wasn't enough human blood left in this place, and if Bartholomew wasn't going to let her heal Quick...

Kulika was far from squeamish, but every time she remembered Quick's face contorted in pain, she winced. She should have known that she was going to run. Even a passing acquaintance with the woman would have been enough to teach her that Quick wasn't the type to sit around and wait, and Kulika and Quick were certainly more than acquaintances.

She'd nearly kissed her, back on the dock. In front of Bartholomew, no less. She couldn't let herself get that close again. She was Bartholomew's, she reminded herself. She had sold herself to him to buy Quick's freedom, and she wasn't going to void the deal she'd worked so hard to broker.

Quick *would* be free.

Until then, Kulika just had to avoid looking her in the eye. If she did, she was going to break and try to take back everything she'd said out in the corridor earlier. Even if that was an option, now would not be the time. Quick didn't need Kulika to be emotional right now. She needed a fighter and a tracker, someone who could find her friend and bring her back unharmed. That was who Kulika would be, even if the teasing scent of Quick's skin was begging her to be someone else.

It didn't take long to find Dr Ross. She'd set up in the kitchen on the other side of the mansion, glass slides littering the countertops as she squinted at one after another through the ancient microscope.

'You left them alone,' Kulika accused, unexpected rage bubbling up inside her. It took her a moment to work out why she was feeling so angry, then she realised: *it could have been Quick*.

'You've got blood on your collar,' the doctor said, looking at Kulika with a mixture of concern and disapproval. 'And you smell like him. Bartholomew.'

'The Primus, you mean.'

'No,' Dr Ross said calmly. 'That's not what I meant at all.' Then she looked Kulika dead in the eye and said, 'Show me your silver.'

'No,' Kulika replied. Then she added, 'Come with me,' and started walking back towards the library.

'Kulika.' The admonishment in Dr Ross's voice was enough to irritate Kulika into turning around.

'I don't answer to you, doctor,' she snapped. 'We don't

even answer to the same master anymore, but right now we need to work together, because Digs has taken Evita.'

The emotions flitted across Dr Ross's face in quick succession: fear, pain, concern. But she didn't move.

'Are you coming?' Kulika demanded.

'Not until you show me your silver.' Dr Ross's jaw was set, her eyes glinting with determination. It was clear she wouldn't easily be put off.

'Fine,' Kulika muttered angrily. 'If that's what it takes.' She relaxed her control and let her silver flood back into her eyes. The sensation was diminished, again. There was a twitching, stuttering feeling in Kulika's eyes, but no feeling of satisfaction followed. It was underwhelming.

Dr Ross examined her eyes, going up on her tiptoes to lean over the counter, then she leaned back and gave Kulika a level look. 'I checked Quick's blood, like you asked. There's nothing wrong with her, though, is there?' she said. 'It's you, or something *he's* doing to you.'

'That's ridiculous,' Kulika said.

'Are you drinking from him?' the doctor challenged her. 'Is that what this is?'

'Why would you ask that?'

Dr Ross raised her eyebrows at Kulika, looked pointedly at the blood on her collar, then back to her eyes.

'His blood shouldn't be able to do that,' the doctor said.

'Yeah, well.' Kulika thought about the control Bartholomew had over the crew, the blood rituals they underwent, and the way it hurt his people to be apart from him. 'His blood shouldn't be able to do a lot of things that it does.'

'Hmm. Do you know who turned him Silver?'

'No,' said Kulika. 'We're wasting time. We need to be going after Evita.'

'And – like you – Evita was turned by Bartholomew. She carries his blood. Digs has drunk from her. There's an addictive quality to Bartholomew's blood, isn't there?' the doctor probed, coming around the counter. She had to look a long way up to look Kulika in the eye, but once she had Kulika trapped under her scrutiny, there was no escaping it. 'It keeps you close,' she said. 'It calls you to him, and that's a little out of the ordinary, isn't it? That's why I'm asking: who turned him Silver?'

Kulika shrugged, pretending she hadn't just been bullied into submission by a tiny Scottish doctor, and said, 'All I know is it happened in the early sixteenth century, on Hispaniola. He doesn't talk about the rest.' People didn't, generally. It was personal.

Dr Ross was murmuring to herself again in that irritating way she had that meant she was working something out in her head, but she wasn't going to fill Kulika in.

'What?'

'Nothing.'

'Doctor,' Kulika said in an admonitory tone. 'Tell me.'

Dr Ross looked Kulika in the eye. 'I only know one bloodline with that kind of power.'

'Just spit it out,' Kulika said irritably.

'Fine,' the doctor replied, with equal irritation. 'I think Bartholomew's bloodline is descended from the Primus – the *real* Primus. Solomon.'

That shut Kulika up.

'With Bartholomew's blood being as powerful as it is,' Dr Ross went on, 'it's the only explanation that makes sense. The timeline works too.'

Kulika looked at her, silently requesting an explanation. It couldn't be true, could it?

'The last Silver that was sired by Solomon,' Dr Ross said,

'the only one I know of, anyway – died in the sixteenth century, in what they called the New World.'

'But that would mean that I…'

'You share blood with the two most powerful Primi in the world. In any world, old or new. Your bloodline is *the* bloodline, and Solomon is your great-grandsire, and Evita's. Since Digs has been drinking from Evita—'

'He now has that blood in his veins too,' Kulika finished.

'Maybe. The properties of a bloodline shouldn't transfer like that, not if the Silver isn't made with them, but then Digs isn't a normal Silver.'

'Shit.'

Kulika ran her fingers through her hair, wondering how they were going to kill Digs if they couldn't use the doctor's formula. Taking the Silver out was no easy matter. The young ones were vulnerable, sure, but once their ages got into the centuries, they were practically indestructible. She supposed they could take him apart, piece by piece, and let the tide take him, but she'd heard of ancient Silver coming back from worse.

She could understand now why Bayly had just locked him away in a box.

'If you keep letting him do this,' Dr Ross said, 'I think he's going to break the bond.'

'What?' Kulika said, not following her train of thought.

'If you keep drinking Bartholomew's blood,' Dr Ross clarified. 'It's going to destroy your bond to Quick. In more ways than one.'

'Which you said would be a good thing, so why are you giving me a hard time about it?' Kulika said.

'I said it would be *easier*, assuming you took the time to think about it and decide whether or not it was what you wanted. I didn't say you should fall into it just because he wants you to. I didn't say it would be *good*.'

'What wouldn't be good?' Quick asked.

Kulika turned around to see her standing with Xiaoyu in the doorway, looking decidedly impatient.

'It wouldn't be good if you hung around much longer,' Kulika said, improvising desperately.

'Yes,' Quick said sharply. 'You've made your thoughts on that perfectly clear. And once we find Evita, you'll never have to see me again.'

Kulika couldn't stand the pain in Quick's eyes. God, how she wanted to take the words back, but she couldn't. She *shouldn't*.

It wasn't too late to get Quick to safety. If she could just get Evita back from Digs, and get them all bundled back on their way to the airport, then everything would be fine. She should have done it hours ago, but then there had been the zombies, and Bartholomew, and now Evita. Still, it was done, and it was done the best way she'd known how at the time. All of it, even the terrible things she'd said. The easiest way to get Quick gone was to push her away, so Kulika had pushed.

It had been necessary.

'You've got the vials?' Kulika asked Dr Ross.

'In the cool bag,' she replied, pointing to where it sat on the counter. 'Remember what I said about Digs's blood.'

'I remember,' Kulika said.

If the doctor's theory was right, then her formula would be completely useless against Digs, but the only way they could know for sure was by testing it, so that's exactly what Kulika intended to do.

'Are Bayly and Enzo still out?' Kulika asked the doctor.

'Yes. They're sleeping upstairs.'

'Under guard?'

'Penny's with them.'

'Hmm.'

That didn't seem like enough. Kulika would send a real guard up there, maybe a couple, with radios. She wouldn't put it past Digs to come back for Bayly if things went wrong with Evita.

'Sun's setting,' Quick reminded her.

'All right,' Kulika replied, leaning over the counter to grab the four remaining full vials from Dr Ross's cool bag. 'Then we're going to need these.'

15

QUICK AND DR Ross followed Kulika through the house to a cupboard by the porch doors, which turned out to be another gun safe. She pulled out four long-barrelled guns from the cabinet and started racking the vials into each of them.

'You know how to use one of these?' she asked Quick.

Quick had never touched a gun in her life, but she said, 'Yes,' anyway, because if everyone else was going to have one, then she wanted one too.

Kulika was not fooled. She gave Quick an unimpressed look – one that had become painfully familiar over the past few hours – opened one of the guns up again and passed the vial inside it to Quick. She didn't let go immediately, though.

'If this breaks,' Kulika said, 'and if it gets into your body, then you're going to burn up. And I'm not just talking about sunburn, I'm talking spontaneous combustion. I won't be able to get to you fast enough to stop it, so please, don't break it.'

'Don't scare the girl,' Dr Ross said, then she turned to Quick and added, 'For what it's worth, I'm fairly certain that your bloodline's immune to it anyway, so I don't think it'll cause you any harm. You, or Kulika, or Evita, for that matter.'

'I'm not relying on that,' Kulika said, with a warning in her voice. 'You haven't tested it.'

'I haven't had time,' the doctor replied. 'You've had me testing *a lot of things,*' she added significantly.

'But it *will* kill Digs?' Quick asked.

'That's the plan,' Kulika said.

Quick did not find her evasive turn of phrase reassuring.

'Here,' said Dr Ross, fumbling in her cool bag for a moment before pulling out a tube with a capped syringe on one end. 'This is easier to use.' She took the vial from Quick's hand and fitted it into the back of the syringe apparatus. 'When you're ready to use it, you just press the end of the vial into the syringe until it clicks, like a cartridge in a fountain pen. Once the vial is loaded, you uncap the needle, stick it into your target, and it'll discharge the formula. Okay?'

Dr Ross handed the syringe to Quick, who took it carefully and stashed it in the pocket of her dress. Not the most practical clothing for hunting vampires, she was prepared to admit, but she hadn't got anything else. It would have to do.

Kulika strapped a radio to her belt, handed one to the doctor, then whistled out of the porch door, and within seconds Phinchas and Wolfrie were standing in front of them.

'Report,' she said.

'He's still doubling back on himself, overrunning old trails,' said Wolfrie. 'Seems to me like he planned it that way, sending off tracks in dozens of directions before he snatched the girl, so we wouldn't know which one to follow when he did.'

'Fuck,' said Kulika. 'You've got people running them down, though?'

'Yup,' said Phinchas. 'Got a pair of the new Silver running each spur to its end, but he's covered a lot of ground. I think we need to search the property again, make sure he hasn't just found a place to hole up here and watch us spin. I want to start at the dock.'

'Then let's do it. You ready?' Kulika asked Quick.

'Ready,' she said, though the bubbling feeling in her stomach said otherwise. She felt sick with anxiety, and exhaustion, and fear. If they didn't get Evita back, if it was too late—

'Hey,' Kulika whispered, taking her hand for a moment. 'We'll find her. I promise you. Now, are you ready?'

How was it that, after all the times Kulika had pushed her away, Quick still felt so settled by her touch? Those points of connection – finger to palm, fingertip to wrist, thumb to thumb – seemed to ground her to the earth in ways she couldn't explain. She still wanted Kulika, much though she might wish she could stop, but there was so much more than that to Quick's feelings. When she was this close to her, breathing her scent and hearing the slow pulse beneath her skin, it was as though Quick's body slowed to keep time with Kulika's.

Joyful synchronicity. Quick had never known anything like it. Together, they just clicked.

Quick took a deep breath and said, 'I'm ready.'

This time, she meant it.

Quick didn't like the mansion at night. It reminded her of when she'd first arrived in this inescapable place, with the pool lights reflecting off the Spanish moss with an eerie blue glow. She should have taken that as the ill omen it was and got herself right back out of here, but then she wouldn't have found Evita, even if she had lost her again now. She wouldn't have found Kulika either, even if she was about to lose her, too.

Kulika and her two generals didn't go slow on Quick's account. It had been days since she'd used her Silver speed for any prolonged stretch of time, and the mouthful of blood she'd had from Xiaoyu wouldn't keep her running like this for long. But for as long as she had it, she'd use it to find Evita.

They started at the ship. The Silver from the block were putting the finishing touches on the stage and seating as they sped past following what Phinchas said was the newest of the trails, back into the trees at an angle to the direction from which they'd come. The route took them downriver, into parts of the property on the far side of the mansion, where Quick had never been before. They ran into Brandon and Monty there.

'The trail splits into three different directions just up here,' Brandon said.

'We've run these two,' Monty said, pointing to the two trails closest to the mansion.

'We'll take the third,' Kulika said. 'Go mark the ones you've already run on the map, then get everyone picking up the other trails from the riverbank. Set up there. We'll follow this one and loop back. Keep your radios on.'

'Yes, Secundus,' said Monty, then he left with Brandon, but not before giving Quick a dirty look.

Quick, Phinchas, Wolfrie and Kulika ran on, and on, in looping circles through the trees, following trails Quick could barely scent, until she felt a pull in her chest that stopped her dead.

'What?' Kulika said, halting the others when she realised Quick was no longer following the pack.

'There's something…' said Quick, but it was such a strange feeling that she didn't know how to put it into words. It was a tugging in the pit of her stomach, like falling in love, or stepping on a stair that wasn't there. It was a horrifying mixture of attraction and repulsion. She didn't know whether she truly wanted to find its source, or if all she wanted was to reassure herself that there was nothing there at all, in the same way she'd felt a compulsion to check for monsters under the bed as a child.

Either way, it drew her irresistibly closer, though at the same time she couldn't work out where it was coming from. From the intensity of the sensation, she should be right on top of it. It was dark in the woods at night, but she had senses that were more than capable of dealing with that. If there was anything here, she should be seeing it.

'I think I can feel her,' Quick whispered.

'Maybe it's the blood,' Kulika suggested.

'What?'

'Bartholomew shared his blood with Evita when he turned her Silver. I shared it with you when I turned you. There's something about his blood: it calls to us.'

'Does that mean you can feel it, too?'

For a moment, Kulika stood still, then her gaze panned upwards into the canopy above Quick's head.

Shit.

It was coming from the trees.

Phinchas and Wolfrie leapt up into the branches, but it was too late, because Digs was already coming down. He landed on the ground in front of Quick, crouching like a tiger, gripping Evita's waist in one sinewy, distorted, gore-rimed arm. She wasn't moving, and even at a moment's glance Quick could see that she was riddled with bite marks. Her head lolled at a terrifying angle; all Quick could see at the spot where her neck joined her shoulder was blood and black filth. If she hadn't been groaning, Quick would have thought she was dead.

The Digs creature hissed, then relinquished its grip on Evita to lunge at Quick. It took her to the ground, digging skeletal digits into her shoulders so hard that they broke the skin. She screamed and tried to push him off, but his open jaws were dripping horror onto her face, rotten liquid that smelled like old blood and dead things. It burned her skin, blistering her like the sun did. She thought for sure that his teeth would be in her neck next, but then Kulika was there, ripping Digs from her body and his fingers from her flesh.

They wrestled for a moment, then the Digs creature leapt back into the treetops, empty-handed this time.

'After him!' Kulika yelled at Wolfrie.

He jumped into the branches after Digs and disappeared into the night. Quick rushed to Evita's side, gathering her into her arms.

'She's alive,' Kulika said to Quick. 'Get her out of here.'

'She can't walk!' Quick looked down at her barely-conscious friend, horrified at the new bites and scratches punched through her clothes and into her flesh. 'She's barely even awake!'

God, there were so many bites. Not just indentations, but pieces of missing flesh.

'Then carry her,' said Kulika. 'Phinchas?'

'I've got her,' he said, scooping Evita gently up into his arms.

'Get her healed,' Kulika said.

'How?' asked Quick desperately. 'The blood cellar's full of nothing but zombies. There's just Xiaoyu, and she can't spare enough blood to heal this much damage.'

'Take her to the ship,' Kulika said after a moment's pause.

'Bartholomew has a human there with him. She can drink from him. Phinchas, make sure they're safe, then come right back here afterwards, okay?'

'You want us to stay on that ship with Bartholomew?' Quick said, horrified.

'No,' Kulika said, already heading off in the direction Wolfrie had gone. 'I want you to get out of here. Digs is our problem. All this is our problem. Get Evita healed, then go straight to the house, collect Xiaoyu and Dr Ross, go to the airport, and fly home.'

'I can't just leave—'

'Go home, Quick.'

'Kulika...'

But she had already followed Wolfrie into the trees. Kulika was gone. Quick looked after her hopelessly. That was to be their final goodbye, then.

'Come on,' Phinchas said quietly. 'Let's get her to the ship, fast.'

Quick turned her back on the spot where Kulika had disappeared, and walked out of the trees with Phinchas carrying Evita at her side.

Go home.

She could try. Maybe this time, she'd be lucky, and she'd finally succeed.

When they arrived at the riverbank, it was buzzing with activity. The stage was fully-constructed now, black-skirted and sombre against the river's surface, which glittered in the moonlight behind it. The stadium-style seating opposite, four rows tall and running the length of the stage, looked large enough to accommodate hundreds of people, and it was plush. No raw wood for this audience; the benches had been upholstered and padded, seat and back, bringing the impression of class and comfort to what had just been bare bleachers earlier in the night. There were even tables built into the structure at regular intervals. The Silver from the block were ornamenting them with flowers and tea lights, and draping them with blood-red satin.

Finishing touches.

Other Silver were running between the driveway on the far side of the lawn and the stage at the riverside, laying a red-carpeted path between the two that was lit with torches. It was a spectacle, luring people towards Bartholomew's stage, which was clearly the main event. As glorious as the ship looked, glinting enticingly in its berth, it was merely the backdrop to the podium that stood centre-stage. Quick could imagine how it would look when Bartholomew was standing there, making his revelations.

But that was not why she was here.

'Can you jump?' she asked Phinchas as they ran down onto the dock, pushing through the bustling crowds of Silver at work.

'To the ship?' he asked. 'Of course. Why? Can't you?'

'Just go,' Quick replied irritably. 'I'll catch up.'

She started hauling herself up the rope ladder. By the time she arrived at the top, Phinchas had laid Evita on the moonlit deck. There were a few Silver up here, polishing the wood and carrying boxes around, but she paid no attention to them. Evita still wasn't moving.

'I don't like the look of those bites,' Quick said, hurrying over to join Phinchas and Evita. They were seeping blood and black goo. 'And I don't want to keep moving her around. Can you radio Dr Ross and ask her to come to us?'

After a brief conversation over the radio, Dr Ross appeared, carrying Xiaoyu, and the two of them started assessing Evita's injuries.

'Multiple lacerations,' Xiaoyu said, twisting Evita back

and forth gently. Her head lolled on her neck, which was so gruesomely mangled that Quick couldn't bear to look at it. 'She's losing what little blood she has left.'

'We're going to need a serious amount to heal her,' said Dr Ross, 'and I've already used everything I had on Bayly and Enzo.'

'I know where we can get more,' Quick said.

'Hey,' said one of the guys from the block. 'You're letting her bleed all over the deck. We just got that cleaned.'

'Then clean it again,' Quick said as she stood and crossed the deck towards him. 'Where's Bartholomew?'

'The Primus?' the guy said uncertainly.

'Do you know another Bartholomew?'

'He's in his cabin,' the guy said, pointing the way, 'but he's preparing his speech for tonight. He said he doesn't want to be disturbed. Hey! You can't go in there!'

The guy tried to stop Quick, but she was a desperate woman on a mission. She batted him aside easily and slammed her way into the cabin.

Bartholomew was sitting at a desk on the far side of the room, writing notes with a fountain pen on a few loose leaves of expensive-looking paper. When Quick barged in, he looked up, his irritated expression morphing instantly into one of undisguised interest.

He looked hungry.

'Patience,' he said with a grin. 'What brings you back to me?'

'Kulika said you had a human here. We need him.'

'Why?'

'For his blood.'

'Clearly, but again, I ask you: why?'

'We found Vee,' Quick explained. 'But Digs drank from her, a lot. She's lost almost all her blood. She's covered in bites, and she's not conscious.'

Was Quick just imagining the concern that flashed across Bartholomew's expression? She was watching for it this time, in a way she hadn't been when she'd seen him almost flinch on the dock earlier, when Kulika had told him that Digs had taken Evita. He masked it quickly with nonchalance, but that little flicker of emotion was enough to make Quick hope that he might actually help.

That hope was crushed the moment Bartholomew opened his mouth.

'Is she going to die?' he said. 'Hardly. She survived weeks in a box with Digs while he continually drank her blood, so it seems unlikely to me that he's done enough damage to her in, what? A half hour? For her to be in any real danger. So explain to me, Patience, if you please: why should I squander the blood of the last viable human on the property to heal her?'

'You turned her Silver,' Quick said incredulously. 'You must have cared about her at least a little to do that. That's what turning someone Silver means, right? All I'm asking you to do is help her.'

'And if I do that,' Bartholomew said. 'What then?'

She hesitated, not immediately understanding what he was getting at, then he slid open the drawer of his desk and pulled out a book. It wasn't the same one that Quick had signed on the night of the Casting, but it was similar enough that she could guess what it was for.

'Are you seriously bargaining with me right now?' she asked.

Bartholomew didn't reply, he just pushed the book across the deck, then sat back in his chair and stared up at her, resting his elbows on the chair's arms and his steepled fingers on his bottom lip.

What were her options, realistically? Quick couldn't put Evita on a plane in the state she was in. She was scared even to move her with her throat all torn up like it was, and she was certain the doctor would object if she tried.

'What's your offer?' she asked, eyeing the book hesitantly.

'I have plans for Aloysius,' Bartholomew said. 'Do you know that he has an encyclopaedic knowledge of my entire life as a pirate, and Kulika's too?'

'So he's a fan?' Quick asked, making clear by her tone just how ridiculous she thought it was that anyone would be a fan of Bartholomew.

'He's an archivist,' Bartholomew replied reproachfully. 'He's wealthy. He's influential. And he's exactly the kind of sponsor and ambassador I can use, so I really will only use his blood as a last resort. Isn't that right, Aloysius?'

Bartholomew looked off to one side, and Quick followed his gaze to a four-poster bed tucked into a recess to her right. There was a middle-aged man sitting on the floor on its far side, tied to one of the bedposts. He was in no position to answer Bartholomew's question, because he was gagged.

'But of course,' Bartholomew continued, 'he is, above all, a storyteller. A bit of a fantasist, true, but such men can be useful. I'm loathe to share him.'

'I'm sorry,' Quick said to Aloysius, 'I don't know you, and I'm sure you're a very nice man, but taking a cup of your blood won't hurt you, and it'll heal my best friend. I've got a doctor up on deck, two actually, and they can—'

Quick stopped talking mid-sentence, her mouth falling open. She'd just noticed the enormous portrait hanging over the bed.

'Is that Kulika?' she asked.

'Of course,' Bartholomew replied. He got to his feet and walked around the desk so he could see it better himself.

Unfortunately, that put him closer to Quick than she would have liked, leaving just a couple of feet between them. 'It's a few centuries old now,' he went on, 'but a good likeness, don't you think?'

It was, admittedly, a good likeness. Kulika looked like the warrior she was, facing down a storm with steely-eyed determination. It was an expression that Quick recognised, and she hated to see it hanging over Bartholomew's bed. The jealousy churned in her stomach, and she wasn't doing a very good job of hiding it.

'She was mine first, you know,' he reminded her. 'And you don't love her, anyway. Anyone could see that plainly enough.' He snatched her face into his hands, too abruptly for Quick to react, then ran a fingertip down her temple and along her jawline. Staring at her the whole time, his grip tightening with every second, he traced the same fingertip up her cheek until it rested just below her eye, close enough to tickle her lower lashes. 'There's nothing in your irises except green. Besides, she signed you away, you know.'

He dropped Quick's face as though it disgusted him, then turned back to the desk. Opening the book, he flicked through the pages until he came to a page that was dense with red ink.

No, not ink. Blood.

Kulika's blood, sea fresh and thick with salt.

'But still,' he said, 'she can't seem to let you go.'

Quick leaned in closer, trying to see what was written on the page, but Kulika's handwriting was dense and choppy. She picked out just a few names and phrases: *a new covenant, Patience Quick, Evita Khalyed, release your claim.*

'And it seems to me,' he continued, 'that you're not entirely ready to leave her either. Are you?'

'All I'm asking for is a little blood,' Quick said. 'I didn't come here to talk about my feelings.'

'Very well,' Bartholomew replied, amused in a way that unsettled her. 'I will give you a little blood, then. But not Aloysius's blood. You'd need half of what's in his body if Digs really has drunk as much as you say, and I won't risk him on that. No. Instead, I'll give you a small measure of my own blood, which I assure you is far more potent than that of any human.'

He made it sound like an upgrade, but there had to be a catch. There was always a catch.

'In return for what?' Quick asked suspiciously.

Bartholomew pushed the book towards her again, opening it to a blank page.

'A cupful of my blood, along with all the healing properties it possesses, in return for your name in my book.'

Quick froze.

'Your friends leave tonight,' he added. 'You stay.'

'I'm not signing your covenant again,' Quick said, horrified. 'I only cut the damned thing out of my skin this morning.'

'Then you shouldn't have come back here, should you?' he said plainly. 'Now, if you don't mind, I have a press conference that's starting shortly, so what is it to be? It's your signature for your friend's health and freedom. Do we have a bargain?'

It was a terrible deal. One cup of blood in exchange for Quick's freedom? But if she didn't make that deal, they'd all be stuck here beyond Bartholomew's grand revelation, and after that Quick was certain there would be no escape, ever again. Evita needed help if she was going to catch a plane out of here tonight, and Quick was determined to make that happen.

She owed it to her friend.

'Pass me the bloody quill,' she said, before she had a chance to second-guess the decision she knew she had to make.

Bartholomew pulled the covenant stamp out of his desk drawer and gave her a smile of such satisfaction that Quick had to restrain herself from ruining their deal by slapping it right off his face.

'As I'm sure you remember,' he said cheerfully, 'this is going to hurt.'

16

IN THE WOODS on the far side of the mansion, Digs was leading Kulika and her generals around and around in circles. At first, he'd been easy to follow. Wolfrie had been right behind him when they'd found Evita, matching him jump for jump as he leapt between the branches, but by the time Kulika had caught up, Digs was already beginning to slip the net. It wasn't long before he was out of sight entirely. They were stuck looking for subtler signs then, picking out broken twigs and smears of black gore, but it was impossible to tell if those marks had been left two minutes or two hours before. They fell behind.

'Left, in the trees,' Phinchas murmured from somewhere behind Kulika. He'd always had a keen nose, and he'd crewed with Digs before Kulika had even been born, so she trusted him to pick out Digs's scent better than most, even if it had now become corrupted by time and god knows what else. If Phinchas had been the one who'd stayed behind with her instead of Wolfrie, maybe they wouldn't have lost Digs by the time he joined them again.

But there was nothing Kulika could do about that decision now. At least she knew Quick was safe.

They tracked Digs like this, following him through the woods slower than Kulika would have liked. He was moving at Silver speed, jumping from one tree to another, but tracking took longer. The more they tracked, the more they lagged behind, until they looped back to the mansion where the trail dead-ended at the tunnel Digs had dug out of the wine cellar.

'Fuck,' Kulika said. 'Did he go in?'

Phinchas crawled his way through the tunnel and popped back out again a few minutes later. 'Locked up tight,' he said. 'The guards in the house didn't see or hear anyone, and they would've done. They were close.'

'Then we must have lost his trail when it crossed another. He hasn't been back here since he got out this morning.'

'Orders?' Wolfrie asked. He got terse when he got irritated, and now that Digs had slipped through their fingers, they were all feeling pretty fucking irritated.

'Back into the woods,' Kulika said, already speeding in that direction herself.

It didn't take long to find the point where they'd gone wrong; fresher black marks stained the trees on the trail they hadn't taken, but those marks had been hidden by dense foliage. Now, approaching from the other direction, they were clear as day.

'This way,' Kulika said.

The others followed, but before long they hit another fork in the scent trail. Kulika stopped and listened, trying to pick out his heartbeat somewhere in the woods, but it was no use. If a normal Silver's heartbeat was slow, then Digs's moved at a glacial pace. Maybe it was something to do with his enforced stasis in that box. He'd been trapped in there for three hundred years before Evita was thrown in there with him, and who knew what transformations his body had gone through during that time? When Evita's blood woke him up – not just any blood, but blood that had inherited power from Bartholomew, and probably from Solomon as well, if Dr Ross was to be believed – it had turned him into a creature unlike anything the world had ever seen before.

Kulika could buy that part of Dr Ross's theory. But the idea that zombie blood had contaminated him with her formula? She wasn't so sure that the drug was responsible for Digs's hunger for Silver flesh. He'd bitten a chunk out of Bayly's leg on the boat at the marina, and he hadn't even come into contact with the zombies by then. Kulika was inclined to believe that Digs had been a monster long before he'd come out of that box.

Which would be convenient, because it would mean the vial loaded into her gun was plenty powerful enough to kill him. If only she could bloody find him.

There was a noise from the direction of the river. This far into the woods, it wasn't more than a faint echo at the edge of Kulika's hearing, a nearly-not-there sound that had her questioning her own senses. But she had heard *something*.

It had sounded worryingly like an interrupted scream.

'Penny,' she said quietly into her radio. 'All quiet with you?'

The radio buzzed, and Penny said, 'All quiet at the house.'

Which was what Kulika had hoped to hear, and yet it worried her.

'Phinchas,' Kulika said as a horrible feeling pooled in her stomach. 'You got Quick and Evita to safety, right?'

'Right,' he said. 'I left them on the ship, like you said.'

'You didn't take them back to the house?' she asked, panicking now. 'You didn't put them in a cab?'

Phinchas looked confused. 'You said to come right back here.'

'I meant *after* you'd— Never mind.'

Kulika spoke into the radio again. 'Do you have Evita and Quick with you?' she asked. 'Did they come to the house?'

'No.'

'They're not with you?' she pressed.

'No,' Penny replied. 'Should they be?'

The horrible feeling in Kulika's stomach became a stone. It weighed so heavily that it threatened to drop her to her knees. Digs couldn't have looped back around again, could he? They'd been following his trail the whole way, so unless he'd somehow got behind them and circled back—

'Shit!' Kulika yelled.

'What?' Wolfrie asked.

She'd made a serious fucking miscalculation.

'Back to the ship!' Kulika called to him and Phinchas, already speeding in that direction herself. 'Right now!'

There had been precious little blood in Evita's veins when they'd found her. She'd been emptied out like a juice box, sucked almost dry. If Digs had gone after her because of her addictive blood – the same blood that ran in Kulika's veins – then he would have no further use for her. But there were two other people on the property with that bloodline, one of them being the person that Kulika herself had turned, the other being the person who had turned her.

And they were both on that ship.

Down by the dock where the *Primus's Fortune* rested, the Silver of the block were standing to attention, eerily still and dressed in their finery as they awaited their guests. It wouldn't be long now. Kulika could hear cars in the driveway back at the house, and wisps of voices were drifting along the red carpet on the breeze towards the moonlit stage. It was very grand, and very beautifully presented, but it held no interest for Kulika. Her eyes were fixed instead on the ship, scouring every varnished surface for a trace of Digs's passage.

Monty was waiting by the rope ladder.

'Hey!' Kulika said to him. 'What happened to the search? You were supposed to be coordinating from here.'

'I got new orders,' he said with a shrug. 'The press are arriving for the party.'

'And what do you think will happen if Digs wanders right into the middle of it?'

'I'm not a complete idiot,' he replied, which was exactly what Kulika was thinking he was. 'I set up a perimeter around the area. He's not getting through.'

'Then what was that scream I heard a minute ago?' Kulika asked.

Monty shrugged and said, 'I don't pry into the Primus's business.' His eyes drifted towards the ship behind him.

That sounded horribly ominous. Kulika could smell Quick's scent, and it was definitely coming from the ship, but it wasn't *right*. The problem wasn't just that Kulika could no longer detect Quick's mood from her changing scent, it was that the core scent itself had almost... soured.

'Where are Quick and Evita?' Kulika asked, dread filling her stomach.

'Last I saw, Dr Ross was carrying Evita along the deck. I guess she got hurt? They were heading for one of the rooms at the back of the ship,' said Monty.

'The "back"?' Kulika asked. The kid had clearly never served on a ship in his life.

'You know,' he said. 'The rooms under the bridge thing down behind where the steering wheel is, with all the windows.'

The sterncastle.

Kulika didn't bother to climb aboard. Instead, she ran

straight along the dock to the stern of the ship, where a balcony protruded out over the water from the captain's cabin. Phinchas and Wolfrie ran with her. Once they were there, they could jump straight up to the balcony and get inside the—

There were smears of black gore on the balcony railing. The windows underneath it were smashed and bloody.

'Wolfrie,' Kulika breathed.

'I see it,' he said, then he was leaping from the dock, hanging off the edge of the balcony by his fingertips, and swinging through the already-smashed windows into the infirmary beyond. Kulika and Phinchas landed beside him in the small room, one after the other, packed in like sardines. It was otherwise empty, but it was clear that it hadn't been that way for long. There was blood on the floor, and blood on the door, and it all smelled like Quick.

Kulika's stomach lurched.

Everything here smelled like Quick, so strongly that Kulika couldn't get a bead on where the woman herself might be. The ship was noisy, and unfamiliar despite its familiarity, so she couldn't work out which creaks were footsteps and which were just the normal sounds the ship made as she settled against the dock. She was panicking.

'Look,' said Phinchas, pointing at a trail of wet black marks, dragged across the cabin floor and out of the door.

'He came through the water,' Kulika said.

'Clever,' Wolfrie commented.

Clever enough to worry Kulika more. The trio followed the tracks into the officers' mess and through it, then down into the cargo hold in the bowels of the ship. That's where they finally found their quarry.

Bayly and Enzo were there, unconscious and bloody against the galley bulkhead. Digs must have brought them here, which explained why she and her generals had followed his trail back to the house: he'd gone back for another bite of his last meal. Dr Ross was lying on the floor beside them, bleeding profusely from a filthy-looking wound that went right through her shoulder and out the other side. Behind her, Evita was standing – conscious, but unsteady – in front of Xiaoyu.

Then there was Digs. He wasn't paying attention to any of the others, because he already had what he wanted in his rotting, skeletal fingers. Quick was pinned up against the hull, her face hidden behind a messy curtain of hair as she twisted and kicked in Digs's grip. Digs's dark mouth salivated in viscous, black drips as he leaned in, his teeth inching ever closer to Quick's neck as she tried in vain to break free. It wasn't a fair fight. Quick had barely drunk enough blood over the past week to replenish her strength, whereas Digs had a belly full of the most powerful bloodline in the world.

He was winning.

Kulika didn't stop to think, she just waded in. Her hands were around Digs's throat, closing over the slimy tendons of his neck and sinking far deeper into his flesh than should have been possible. Under the disintegrating scraps of his clothes and whatever rotting shreds of skin he'd retained, Digs was a construct of bone, bare muscle and raw nerves.

'Get them out of here!' Kulika yelled to Phinchas and Wolfrie.

'You sure you don't want us to—' Phinchas started.

'Just do it! Get them up top!'

Kulika hooked one arm around Digs's neck, then climbed onto his back and reached out to unhook his fingertips one by one from the spots where they had embedded themselves bloodily into Quick's shoulders, reopening the wounds he'd made earlier this evening. He threw Kulika off within a few seconds, but by that time Quick was free too, falling down the inside wall of the ship's hull to crumple into a pile on the floor. When Kulika glanced to the side, the other injured Silver and Xiaoyu had all disappeared, along with Phinchas and Wolfrie.

Now she had space to make some mess.

But fighting Digs this time wasn't like it had been back on Bayly's boat. Then, he'd been blood-starved and weakened by three hundred years in a box, so wrestling him back into it had been a piece of cake. Now, full of stolen blood and hungry for more, he moved less like a wraith and more like a demon; with purpose.

Kulika realised then that the problem with sending her generals away with the wounded was that it meant the people left in the room were exactly the ones Digs wanted: the ones with Bartholomew's blood. But it was too late to regret her choices now. Digs was already hurling himself across the cargo hold towards her, a snarling morass of dripping black claws and sharp teeth. He thudded into her with the speed of a cannonball and took her to the deck just as hard, slamming her against the planks so forcefully that they splintered underneath her shoulders, along with a couple of her ribs. She grunted and pushed back, managing to flip him over so she had the upper hand.

Then Quick groaned.

Kulika shouldn't have looked. She was in the middle of a fight with a supercharged and cannibalistic Silver. She should have given him her full attention, but she couldn't resist the urge to look and see if Quick was all right. In the split second it took for Kulika to ascertain that no, Quick was not all right – in fact she was bleeding out against the bulkhead – Digs was on her again. This time, he didn't just flip Kulika, he hauled her to her feet and spun her around, then pinned her against the hull with one hand to her sternum. With the other, he reached down and grabbed Quick, then pinned her to the hull next to Kulika, lining them up on a level with his jaws.

Kulika was left staring into the wrecked remains of Digs's face.

His skull wasn't as misshapen as it had been, nor was the rest of his body. He'd already amply demonstrated that he could move as fast as the rest of the Silver, and he was stronger than Kulika had expected, even if his gait was strange and his limbs were deformed.

But his face. Up to this point, Kulika hadn't looked at it closely. Now, she could see that his blank white eyes were in the process of healing, but they were growing back wrong. Eyeballs that should have been uniformly round were sitting twisted and bulbous in their sockets. His mouth wasn't much better formed, with a half-healed tongue that lolled inside a mouth whose innards were always visible through his cheeks, only half-covered by skin and tendon.

For a moment, Kulika was too horrified to do anything. She wasn't sure how long she might have stared into Digs's shredded maw if she'd been on her own in his grip, but Quick was there beside her, and she wasn't down just yet. She was fumbling for her pocket, the one where she'd stashed the syringe full of the doctor's formula. Kulika's gun containing her dose of the same had been batted aside with Digs's first attack, but it would be useless at this close range anyway. Quick's syringe was precisely the weapon they needed. The problem was that Quick seemed to be having trouble gripping it, as though her hand wasn't working quite right. If Kulika could just inch her hand along the hull and…

Kulika's fingers brushed the syringe. It was at the very

edge of her reach. She scissored it between her fingers, then teased it out of Quick's pocket as quickly and gently as she could, flicking it up into her fist. But in the instant before she could inject the syringe's contents into the remains of Digs's stomach, he spotted the movement with his roaming eyes and stabbed a sharp fingernail into Kulika's arm. Her fist unravelled, unintentionally, and the syringe clattered to the ground, unused.

That wouldn't have been the end of it, Kulika told herself. She would have got her and Quick out of the situation one way or another, but she never had a chance to find out exactly how she was going to do that, because at that moment Bartholomew breezed down the stairs from the upper decks and came up behind Digs. Kulika could have saved them both, she was almost certain, but it was Bartholomew who *actually* did. He reached out and grabbed Digs's head in one hand, then twisted it sharply until it snapped with a sickening crunch.

Digs dropped both Kulika and Quick, and while he was writhing on the floor trying to put himself back together, Kulika snatched up her gun from where it had fallen. She shot Digs in the stomach, where his broken body was thickest, and Dr Ross's formula did its job.

Thank god.

It started in his stomach, where the dart containing the vial had embedded itself, a spreading glow of red. At first, it looked like blood pooling around the wound, but then the colour intensified through red to orange to yellow to white as it filtered out through Digs's body. The surface of his mutilated muscles hardened over it like porcelain, forming a baked black crust where his skin should have been. That skin cracked open, creating a multitude of fault lines that pulled apart to reveal white-hot emptiness inside his trunk and limbs, then there was nothing except a pile of ash and a charred circle on the planks to mark the spot where his body had burned.

It was over in just a couple of seconds, but the flashing glare was burned into the backs of Kulika's eyes for far longer.

Digs hadn't been a creature like Jahan Khalyed, then. He hadn't been contaminated by the zombie blood, and however much of Evita's blood he had in his body, it hadn't been enough to protect him from the formula in the doctor's vials.

Kulika rushed to Quick's side. Bartholomew watched her go.

'You killed him?' Quick asked Kulika in a broken whisper. 'He's properly dead?'

'Yes,' Kulika promised.

'You're welcome,' Bartholomew interjected, with a smile in his tone.

Kulika looked over her shoulder as she cradled Quick in her arms and asked, 'Are you expecting my thanks? You should never have brought him here in the first place.'

'I had a use for him,' Bartholomew replied nonchalantly.

'*Had*?'

'As I told you,' Bartholomew said as he flicked Dig's black ichor from his fingers, 'I've got everything I wanted from him.'

'And what exactly did you want?' Kulika asked.

But Bartholomew didn't answer the question, he just smiled and said, 'It's good to have the crew back together, isn't it? And now that Digs is dealt with, I have a revolution to incite.' He looked disdainfully at his blackened fingertips and the drips staining his sleeves. 'After I've changed.'

Then he stalked back up the steps as though nothing had happened.

Kulika put him out of her mind and turned her attention to Quick, whose blood was pooling on the boards of the cargo hold. Kulika was kneeling in it, feeling it sink into the material that covered her shins. Quick was still bleeding, albeit slowly. She wasn't healing, either. When Kulika pulled Quick across her thighs and tried to get a better look at the wounds Digs had punched through her chest with his fingers, her faint moan of pain was quiet enough to worry Kulika more.

Well, Bartholomew hadn't told her she *couldn't* heal Quick, had he? He'd known she was injured, and he'd left her here alone with Kulika. What did he think she was going to do, with no blood available?

Tacit permission, Kulika thought. Or as close as made no difference.

Kulika pushed her fingertips into Quick's hair, curving her hand around the nape of her neck until she could feel the thick gathering of Quick's locks between her fingers. The weight of it in her grip settled the anxiety twitching through her muscles as she sent her healing strength through her palm and into Quick's skin, pushing it out through her body until the wounds at Quick's shoulders began to seal themselves shut.

It felt like coming home.

If Kulika could have kissed Quick then, she would have done, but it would only have made what was to come more painful, so she held herself back. With difficulty.

'All right?' Kulika asked as Quick pushed herself first to her elbows, then up to sitting, and finally to her feet.

For a moment, Kulika just sat on the floor and let herself bask in Quick's presence. Standing over Kulika like that, bloodstained and ready for a fight, with her flame-red hair spreading over her shoulders like a cloak of fire, she was glorious.

One last moment, Kulika told herself. Then she'd give her up for good.

'I'm fine, thanks. Are you all right?' Quick asked, giving Kulika a strange look. It snapped Kulika into action, and to her feet.

'I'm fine. We've got,' Kulika checked the time on her phone, 'less than fifteen minutes before the event starts, and the press are already here. Let's get up on deck and find the others.'

<h1 style="text-align:center">17</h1>

QUICK FOUND HER friends in the middle of the ship, by the biggest mast, arguing. Xiaoyu and Evita were trying to get back downstairs while Wolfrie and Phinchas held them back. Dr Ross was lying on the floor, bleeding profusely from her shoulder while she tried to tend to Bayly and Enzo, both of whom were still unconscious.

'You've got to let me back down there!' Evita was yelling. 'She needs me.'

'You can barely stand up straight,' Wolfrie pointed out.

'Maybe she can't,' Xiaoyu said, 'but *I'm* fine. I can go help.'

'No, you bloody can't,' Phinchas said with horror in his voice. 'You're human. It's not safe.'

Then Evita's gaze landed on Quick, coming up from below deck, and her face sagged with relief.

'Oh, god,' she said, pushing past Wolfrie to pull Quick into her arms. 'You're okay? You're not hurt?'

'I'm fine,' Quick said.

'Digs?'

'Dead,' said Kulika.

Quick couldn't stop her gaze from sliding sideways

towards Kulika, wondering whether her body was still rushing with desire the way Quick's was. If so, she was hiding it well. But there was a slight flush to her cheeks, a sparkle in her eyes, and an edge to the ocean salt of her scent that was driving Quick to distraction. Taken together, those three things gave her pause for thought.

Then Kulika said, 'You all need to leave, right now.' She was looking at Quick as she spoke, then she turned to Wolfrie and Phinchas and said, 'Get Bayly and Enzo down to the infirmary, then come right back here. Doctor: hang on, and I'll find you some blood.'

Then Kulika disappeared below decks with her generals, each of whom was carrying an unconscious Silver.

Quick felt empty as she watched them go. Kulika wanted her to leave with the others, but she couldn't. She was bound to Bartholomew as much as Kulika was now, and she was stuck here in exactly the same way. Whatever events Bartholomew was about to set in motion with his speech, she was in it for the long haul.

Kulika was not going to be pleased when she found out.

'Whatever reason you think she has for sending you away, she's not doing it because she doesn't want you,' Evita said quietly, misreading the cause of Quick's concern. 'She loves you. That's the end of that. That's what silvering means, and it's forever.'

'Usually,' Dr Ross muttered, barely loud enough for Quick to hear. Maybe Quick wasn't supposed to hear at all, but she did.

'What does that mean?' she asked.

'Sorry?' the doctor said, turning towards Quick. She'd been looking at her wound, apparently engrossed in her own thoughts and her own pain. Maybe her comment had nothing to do with Kulika.

'You said *usually*,' Quick said. 'Usually what?'

'Usually…' the doctor started, but she didn't seem to know how to finish the sentence. 'Oh, fuck it. Look, something's wrong with Kulika. I don't know exactly how, and I didn't even know it was possible, but the silvering is reversing.'

'Excuse me?' Quick whispered.

'In the circumstances, it's probably a good thing,' Dr Ross said gently. 'You're leaving, and with everything that's happening, you'd be better off if the bond was gone. You don't actually *want* her life to be tied to yours, do you?'

'My life to—' Quick spluttered. 'What are you talking about?'

'If you die, she dies,' the doctor replied.

'You didn't know that either?' Xiaoyu said.

'You *did*?' Quick asked.

'Well, yeah.'

'Assume I know nothing,' Quick said, sitting on the deck beside the doctor. 'Then tell me everything I need to know about what happens when someone silvers.'

She'd barely had a chance to digest the facts she'd been missing before Kulika returned, tossing a plastic drinks bottle filled with blood to Dr Ross.

'Where did you get that from?' Quick asked.

'Same place you did,' Kulika replied. 'Bartholomew's human historian. Aloysius.'

Quick felt like she was going to be sick.

'What?' Kulika asked her.

Quick just shook her head. She'd have to tell the truth eventually, probably very soon indeed, but for now the nausea was so thick in Quick's throat that she wouldn't have been able to get the words out, even if she'd wanted to.

Bartholomew had tricked her. Of course he had. He could

have given her Aloysius's blood for Evita, but he'd spun a sob story and made her trade her freedom for his own blood instead. She felt like a complete fool. It seemed so obvious now, in retrospect, that she couldn't bear to admit how easily she'd been conned.

'Okay,' Kulika said once Dr Ross had drunk the blood and healed her injury. 'Now you need to go.'

'We haven't had time to call a cab, and with the blood—' said Dr Ross, looking hopelessly at the stains on her clothes.

'Grab a clean shirt from the house, then take one of the cars,' said Kulika. 'Leave it at the airport. Get straight into your private plane and fly out of here. Just go, now, before it's too late.'

She was looking straight at Quick as she spoke, but Quick couldn't leave. Evita and Xiaoyu, though? They were free.

'She's right,' Quick said, moving to stand alongside Kulika. 'You should go.'

'Impatience,' Evita said, looking between Quick and Kulika. 'What are you doing?'

'I'm staying,' she replied.

'No, you're not,' said Kulika. 'You can't be here when Bartholomew makes his announcement. All hell's going to break loose. You'll be right in the middle of it. You'll be stuck like the rest of us.'

'I'm still staying,' Quick replied.

Kulika's face was a picture of pained incomprehension.

'No,' said Kulika, anxious now, 'you're not. You're going to run to the utility room, take the first set of car keys you find on the rack, then drive out of here as fast as you can without looking back. You're going, Quick. Right now.'

Quick didn't reply. She didn't know how to say the words. Instead, she just held out her hand, slowly unfurling her fingers to reveal the ugly black mark that scarred her palm.

Again.

'No,' Kulika whispered.

'Evita needed blood,' Quick said.

'What did you do?' Evita asked, her shaky voice full of disbelief.

'You needed blood,' Quick repeated. 'Bartholomew said… Well, it doesn't matter. I got the blood, but he made me sign his book.'

'No!' Evita yelled, tears already starting down her cheeks. She was so upset that she was angry, and it tied Quick's stomach in knots. 'I would have been fine! We could have found more blood. You didn't need to trade for it with Bartholomew! It wasn't worth your freedom. If I'd known —'

'I thought it was the only way to get you home,' Quick said calmly. 'And that's exactly what I'm doing now. If you get on that plane safely tonight, it'll all have been worthwhile.'

'No,' Evita said.

'Yes. It was the right decision at the time. I don't regret it.' Quick crouched down beside her friend and pulled her into her arms, kissed each of her cheeks, then held her tightly for a moment before pushing her away. 'Now go on. Make it mean something,' she begged. 'Please. *Please*.'

Evita just shook her head, crying with her teeth clenched.

'Here,' Quick said. She took the syringe she'd collected from the cargo deck out of her pocket and passed it to Dr Ross, but the doctor curled Quick's fingers back around the vial.

'Keep it,' she said quietly. 'You might still need it.'

Her gaze landed somewhere over Quick's shoulder.

'If you'll excuse me, ladies,' Bartholomew said, worming his way through their group to reach the rope ladder that led down to the dock. It was a pointless interruption; he didn't need to use the ladder. He was more than strong enough to jump the short distance from anywhere along the edge of the ship. He just wanted to rub his triumph in their faces.

Kulika had been standing off to one side up until now, arms crossed and attention fixed on the floor, but now she snapped up straight, her eyes narrowing on Bartholomew.

'We had a bargain,' she said to him, biting out the words.

'And I made another that superseded it,' Bartholomew shrugged, with infuriating calmness. 'I thought you might be pleased, even. After all,' he grinned, 'now you match.' Then he took a long step off the side of the ship and disappeared from view.

'Get them gone, Phinchas,' Kulika said when he and Wolfrie returned, her voice hollow. There was cold rage in her tone.

Quick finished her goodbyes with a briskness that tore at her, hugging Evita while she wept until all the others had already left, and she could delay their parting no longer. Evita followed them down the rope ladder without saying a single coherent word.

Up on the deck, Kulika stood beside Quick and watched as the group moved quickly along the red carpet to the mansion. A few minutes later, an SUV pulled away from the drive in the distance, and then they were gone. Quick had thought they might talk then, but instead Kulika turned and jumped down to the dock without a backward glance, following Bartholomew to the stage. Wolfrie went after her, leaving Quick alone on the *Primus's Fortune*.

Evita was gone. Xiaoyu was gone. The bond between her and Kulika would apparently soon be gone too, but Quick was stuck here forever, come what may.

Alone.

18

'GOOD EVENING, AND welcome,' Bartholomew said from the podium.

Kulika stood behind him on the stage and glared at his back.

Most of the well-dressed crowd had already taken their seats, but those who hadn't now hurried to grab their glasses and find a good vantage point from which to take their pictures. When Bartholomew had told Kulika that he was holding a press conference, this was not what she had expected. She'd imagined there would be cameras and reporters with microphones, poised and ready to ask difficult questions, but of course that was not the crowd he had assembled. Instead, his audience was filled with influencers and internet celebrities, people who'd brought just their phones and their beautiful selves to disseminate the information they were going to learn this evening.

It was a good strategy. Bartholomew had always been skilled at playing his cards to his best advantage. Just look at how he'd played her: he'd got Kulika to sign his covenant by agreeing to break his covenant with Quick, then he'd fed Kulika his blood to reverse her silvering, so he could have her all to himself. But that wasn't enough for him, was it? Nothing was ever enough for Bartholomew. No, he had to have Quick as well, just in case, so he'd found a way to talk her into signing his covenant again. He was as greedy and vicious as the alligators that lived in the river bordering his property. He'd snapped her up in his jaws, then he'd stored her in his larder, playing with her occasionally, until he had need of her.

Tonight, finally, it was time.

With the new Silver slotted in amongst the guests to host and seduce them – Silver who were just as shiny and camera-ready as their guests – the evening felt more like an exclusive cocktail party than a declaration of war. Which was what it actually was.

'Thank you all for coming,' Bartholomew said, holding his hands up as he waited for everyone to settle and take their seats.

He had dressed the part. Gone were the bloodstained jeans and henley from their battle with Digs. Instead, he was now wearing a plain black suit and white shirt, a simple outfit that was understated, yet so well fitted that it gave Bartholomew a subtle aura of power.

Maybe that was just his blood talking.

Kulika's own blood was thundering in her ears. If she could have killed Bartholomew for what he'd done to Quick then she would have done, but every time she thought about making a move, she got this stabbing pain above her eye that didn't subside until she thought about something else. It wasn't part of any Silver lore she'd ever heard of, but it felt as though his blood had poisoned her thoughts themselves. Her own body was conspiring against her, for his benefit, and all the while Quick felt further and further away.

Kulika still felt the tug in her chest that pulled her towards

Quick's spot up on the ship's deck behind her, but the tug was getting weaker. Healing her earlier had been harder than Kulika wanted to admit, harder than it ever had been before. It was as though a barrier had been erected between the two of them, so Kulika could only experience Quick through smoked glass: her scent dulled, her emotions indiscernible, her light muted. She was slipping through Kulika's fingers, and Kulika was just standing back and letting it happen.

Because of him.

As Bartholomew smiled at his audience – who were all smiling back, already suckered in – a few stragglers approached from the driveway, following the torches along the red carpet. Kulika hadn't heard any late cars pulling up, but perhaps the stragglers had stopped at the mansion to use the bathroom before joining the party. They were all dressed appropriately, so they didn't strike her as strange at the time, which was how they got almost halfway to the stage before she realised that something was wrong.

Their movement was odd, that was the first thing she noticed. They swayed and rocked as they walked, but in unison, as though they were dancing to a song only they could hear. Then Kulika thought to look at their eyes, and she saw the bloody tears just beginning to form in the corners of their eyes.

'Shit,' she murmured. Then she yelled for Wolfrie to back her up, and she ran.

There were only five of them, enough for Kulika and Wolfrie to handle on their own, but by that point the audience had turned and seen exactly what was slavering in their direction. For the moment, they were just confused, thinking perhaps it was some kind of stunt, but if Kulika didn't contain the zombies quickly, then the mood would turn.

'Monty!' she yelled.

The kid had been standing at the back of the stage with Kulika and the other favoured Silver, but he arrived immediately. Across the space that separated them, Bartholomew gave Kulika a look that told her she'd better sort this out, right now.

'Back to the cellar,' Kulika ordered.

Monty waved Brandon and Penny over from the stage to join them, then the five of them escorted one zombie each to the block. Now the creatures were under control, with startling ease, Kulika was finally getting a good look at them, and she didn't like what she was seeing. They were dressed in black tie, they were clean and well-presented, and they certainly didn't look like they'd spent the day rambling around mindlessly in the woods.

'They didn't escape from the cellar, did they?' Kulika asked.

'I doubt it,' Monty replied. 'I've got people guarding the block.'

This proved to be true when they dragged the zombies across the lawn and into the building, where they found a Silver standing in the corridor right outside the hidden door that led to the cellar hatch. It was sealed tight.

'Then where did they come from?' Kulika asked as the new zombies were manhandled into the cellar with the rest. 'I thought you said you got them all.'

'We did!' Monty replied, indignantly. 'But there was blood in the wine cellar, and on the grass, probably in the woods too, which we tried to clean up but, you know…'

'We *did* clean it up,' Wolfrie replied. 'There's no blood left on this property.'

'Then on the road,' Monty replied. 'There must have been a lot of blood out there. You said there was a car crash and

that some driver got turned zombie, so there must have been
—'

'Two drivers,' Kulika said, her stomach falling. 'Two
drivers, Monty. One from Quick's cab and one from the
pick-up truck that hit it.'

For a moment, no one said anything, and all they could
hear was the gentle shuffling of the zombies in the cellar
below them.

Then Monty said, 'Oh.'

'Fucking hell,' Kulika muttered. Her voice was low and
tight with barely-controlled rage. 'Everyone back outside.
Now.'

That's when the screaming started.

From her perch on the deck of the *Primus's Fortune*, Quick
had a good enough view to know exactly what kind of
creatures had just been bundled into the block by Kulika and
her helpers. She was also perfectly-placed to see Evita and
Xiaoyu's SUV barrelling back down the drive the same way
it had left, before careening right past the pool and over the
lawn, then finally screeching to a stop behind the tiered
seating that now held Bartholomew's audience. By the time
Dr Ross, Evita and Xiaoyu tumbled out of it, Quick had
already reached the dock.

She heard Bartholomew calling, 'If you'll please remain
in your seats, ladies and gentlemen…' before another zombie
rounded the corner from the mansion, following the trail the
SUV had left from the drive to the riverside. There were ten
others behind it, then fifty, then a hundred, all of them
running, then Quick lost count as she rushed to the SUV.

'Ladies and gentlemen…' Bartholomew was calling, but it
was no use. His audience had seen the zombies too. They
might have hesitated in their seats as the first batch was
escorted away, but they were not going to sit and wait for

who knew how many hundreds of zombies to engulf them.

They screamed. They ran, tripping over heels and hems. They generally got in the way as Quick tried to reach her friends, but they had no real direction, and Quick knew exactly where she was going.

'What are you doing here?' Quick asked, horrified to see Xiaoyu once again in harm's way.

'Did you really think we'd get out?' Evita laughed bitterly.

Then there was no more time for talking, because the zombies had arrived, and they weren't keeping their distance from the Silver anymore, not like they had that morning. There was no ten-foot radius, no safe zone. They were coming straight for Xiaoyu, pushing Silver out of the way to get to her, with no consideration for their strength. Whether the formula had mutated, or things had changed now it was dark, or the zombies had simply got hungrier and more daring as their meals became scarcer, the Silver were clearly no longer a source of fear for them.

Quick and the others were going to have to fight tooth and nail to get Xiaoyu out of here alive.

When Kulika and the others stepped out of the block, it was already too late. There were zombies all over the lawn.

Tyre-treads were gouged either side of the red carpet, following a trail of lanterns knocked over and smouldering gently in the dry grass, leading to an SUV parked behind the seating area.

No.

But there they were, clustered behind the SUV: Evita, Dr Ross and Xiaoyu, with Quick at their side, desperately trying to fend off the zombies that were already beginning to surround them.

'Protect the humans!' Kulika barked to the others. 'Get them on the ship and keep the zombies off it.'

'You don't want to put them in the cellar?' Monty asked.

Kulika gave him an incredulous look and said, 'No.'

There were thousands of zombies on the property already, streaming from the road and the woods in an endless deluge. Even if they could get them all in the cellar and protect the humans at the same time, they would never fit. It would be a futile effort. The only possible solution was to get the humans somewhere safe, and worry about the zombies later.

'You have your orders!' Kulika barked, then she rushed to the SUV, and to Quick.

'Protect Xiaoyu!' Quick yelled the moment Kulika joined them.

'We need to move her somewhere safe,' Kulika said. 'Dr Ross, can you get her on the ship? We'll clear your path.'

The doctor nodded, then Xiaoyu climbed onto her back. It looked a little comical because of Dr Ross's height, like an adult trying to ride a Shetland pony, but the doctor was plenty strong enough to carry one human. While she ran towards the dock with Evita clearing the way, Quick and Kulika fell into position behind the piggybacking pair, moving back to back as they fended off zombies from either side. Kulika should have been concentrating on protecting their precious human cargo, but instead she couldn't stop thrilling at the pressure of Quick's back against her own. There was the push of an elbow against her waist as Quick neatly tossed a zombie away, the brush of a shoulder as she turned to face a new challenger, and the press of hip and flesh as they leaned back against each other for support. It reminded Kulika of the time they'd spent sparring on the training ground – a time that seemed so long ago now that it might have happened in another lifetime – and she warmed at the memory, whilst simultaneously feeling that something was terribly wrong. That smoked glass still spread between them, even when there was nothing between them at all. It was a relief in more ways than one when they reached the ship, and Dr Ross leapt up to the deck safely with Xiaoyu in her arms.

'Go with them,' Kulika said to Quick and Evita.

'But we can help here,' Quick argued.

'You can help by keeping the ship safe for the humans I'm about to send your way. Get up there and guard it, okay?'

'Okay,' Quick said.

Quick reached out, and for a moment Kulika thought she was going to take her hand, or cup her face, or touch her in some other exquisitely tantalising way, but then Quick snatched her hand back, turned without word and started climbing the rope ladder, with Evita close behind. Kulika didn't have time to obsess over what might have happened in that moment, because on the riverbanks, everything was going tits up.

The Silver were everywhere now, trying to form a line behind the tiered seating under the direction of one of the older crew so they could push the zombies back towards the road with brute force. The problem was that there might have been a hundred or so Silver on the property who were each hundreds of times stronger than the zombies, but they were seriously outnumbered. They only had one set of hands each, so when the zombies got backed up behind the barricade of bodies and started climbing over each other to breach the line and reach the humans beyond, there was no one left to catch them. They had a clear field ahead of them, and just a few Silver to pick them off. When the wave of zombies broke over the Silver barricade en masse, there was no holding it back.

On the stage, Bartholomew stood still beside his lectern. He was watching the humans running and screaming, watching the zombies chasing them, watching and watching and doing nothing at all.

'Bartholomew!' Kulika yelled at him.

He turned towards her, then shrugged and called, 'Just let them have the humans. Clear up afterwards, when they've calmed down. It'll be easier that way.'

Which was true, but it was an idea that never would have occurred to Kulika. Let all these people die, for nothing? That was the difference between her and Bartholomew.

But not all the crew were of her mind. The older ones were already gathering beside Bartholomew on the stage, standing in eerie stillness as they watched the carnage churn around them.

Bartholomew shouted, 'Call me when it's over, and we'll start again,' then he walked off towards the mansion with a crowd of nonchalant Silver following on behind.

Kulika gaped after him.

He seriously thought they'd be able to salvage something from this mess? That they could just gather up thousands and thousands of unkillable zombies and, what? Stash them in every waterlogged cellar in the Low Country? He'd had crazier ideas, Kulika supposed, but she didn't have much faith in their ability to turn the tide.

Meanwhile, the audience was dispersing in all directions. A few had locked themselves inside the SUV, but the zombies had already managed to shatter one window, and it wouldn't be long before they were inside. Some ran behind the stage and along the dock, which was where Kulika wanted them to go, but others ran along the river in both directions, where zombies leapt from the rushes and the darkness under the trees to drag them into the water.

'Fuck,' Kulika muttered to herself. 'This isn't good.'

Wolfrie raced past carrying two humans under each arm.

As he passed Kulika, he said, 'Things are getting out of control.'

Which was an understatement.

'Get on the ship!' she yelled, herding whatever part of the audience remained towards the *Primus's Fortune*. 'Cast off!' she called to Wolfrie.

'Aye, aye!' he yelled back.

Kulika gathered the last few humans in her own arms and carried them up to the deck, then helped the remainder who were still climbing the rope ladder to reach safety before pulling the ladder up onto the deck so the zombies couldn't follow.

There had been over a hundred humans in the audience. They were sailing away with maybe thirty.

'Anyone Silver who's coming with us,' Kulika yelled from the bowsprit, leaning out over the water, 'you'd better get on board now!'

From where Kulika was standing, it seemed overwhelmingly unlikely that Bartholomew was going to get the calm zombie clean-up he'd been banking on. She couldn't see a single human left in the mass of bodies moving on the riverbanks now, but the zombies weren't giving up. They were chasing in either direction along the river, looking for new prey, and some of them were even going after the remaining Silver, those who hadn't followed Bartholomew back to the mansion. The last few crew members who leapt onto the ship as they pulled away from the dock had scratches gouged onto their faces and bite marks on their arms.

Kulika was fairly certain there would be no starting again from this, for any of them.

The lawn was on fire. It was already catching in the dry Spanish moss, chasing up into the tree branches and blowing onto the block. In the distance, Kulika could see the porch of the mansion smouldering. The whole place was going to go up in flames.

Just like she'd always wanted.

With any luck, there'd be no mansion left to come back to, and Kulika could just sail off into the sunset. The thought gave her a frisson of glee.

If Bartholomew was angry about her scratching up his car, just imagine how angry he'd be when he realised she'd taken his ship.

19

THE *PRIMUS'S FORTUNE* cruised down the Cooper River, picking up stragglers as it went. A few of the left-behind Silver were following it now as the zombies chased them along the waterside, then diving into the water before hauling themselves up onto the deck. The moment they hit the boards, they came face to face with Kulika and Wolfrie, who were shouting orders Quick didn't understand.

They used to be pirates, Kulika had told her. Well, she was seeing the evidence of that now.

But the Silver weren't the only figures in the water; the zombies were following them in. They didn't seem to have the strength to pull themselves up the sides of the ship, or maybe they just hadn't yet worked out how, but Silver were patrolling the sides of the boat all the same.

'Where are we going?' Quick asked Kulika.

'Out into the harbour,' she replied, 'for now.'

Then one of the ropes got tangled in a way that made Kulika frown, and she rushed off to fix it, leaving Quick with the distinct feeling that they didn't have much of a plan at all. Quick was no use up here, though. All she was doing was getting in the way, so she went below decks to the space where cannon and hammocks crowded in the centre of the ship. The others were waiting there, peering out of the cannon ports with worried faces.

'They're in the water,' Evita said as Quick hopped up into the hammock across from hers.

'I know,' Quick replied.

'Not just in the water,' said Dr Ross.

She was looking at the screen of her phone, but she turned it then to show Quick a news broadcast. It cut from CCTV footage of downtown Charleston, to the waterfront, and then to the airport. All of the shots were filled with zombies.

Quick took the phone from the doctor's hand and watched in horror as images and text scrolled across the screen, before it abruptly went black.

'Battery's dead,' Quick said, handing it back.

'I don't think so,' Dr Ross said, fiddling with it for a moment before bringing up a lock screen. 'We've lost signal. Maybe we're too far away from a tower out here.'

'But we're still on the river.'

Dr Ross just shrugged and put the phone back in her pocket.

'Just one stowaway, one smear of blood on a plane flying out of here,' said Evita, 'and the whole world is fucked.'

'We know,' said Xiaoyu. 'You don't have to say it.' She was sitting in a hammock on the other side of the ship, swinging gently as she looked out of the cannon port.

When Quick saw Evita glance in that direction, she murmured, 'Her kids live in Charleston, remember?'

Evita looked at Quick with wide eyes, then at Dr Ross, who was nodding sadly.

'You couldn't get through, I guess?' Quick asked. 'Is that why you came back?'

'Road was blocked with zombies,' Xiaoyu said, still

looking out of the window. 'We had no choice.'

'Not that I would have been able to leave anyway,' Evita said bleakly. 'The minute we got more than a mile down the road, I felt like my head was about to explode. We were just turning around when we saw the zombies.'

'We had to turn back,' Dr Ross said quietly. 'I think it was the blood.'

'The blood?' Quick said, confused for a moment before she realised what Dr Ross meant. 'Bartholomew's blood made Evita's head hurt?'

'I think so,' Dr Ross said quietly. 'When she got too far away from him. He knows what his blood can do better than any of us, and he wanted Evita to drink it, to keep her close, I think.'

The conniving bastard. That's why he'd bargained with Quick for his own blood instead of Aloysius's. He'd wanted Evita to come back to him.

'And worse,' Dr Ross went on. 'I think he probably made sure that Digs would get loose in the first place. He sent him after Evita, to keep her at the mansion. To keep you both there.'

'I suppose we'd better hope the zombies keep Bartholomew busy for a while, then,' Quick commented.

'Why?' Evita asked.

'Because otherwise, he might decide he wants us back.'

Up on deck, Kulika was taking stock of her new crew. They'd stowed the humans in the cargo hold for now, as far away from danger as they could get. Kulika had been careful not to mention what exactly had caused the scorch mark on the floor. There were twenty-odd Silver up on deck – including Monty, Brandon and Penny – but only a few of them knew what they were doing on a ship like this, and that wasn't even half the number she'd need to teach the others what they needed to know. She could do with having Phinchas here to help, but he hadn't come up on deck yet. Still, they were muddling along for the moment. All they had to do was let the current take them as far as the harbour. After that, they could…

Well, Kulika didn't know what they were going to do then. She was bound to Bartholomew, like the rest of the crew, but if the mansion had just gone up in smoke, what was she supposed to do now? She'd call Bartholomew if she could, but her phone wasn't working, and nor was anyone else's. He didn't have a radio – hated using them – so she couldn't contact him that way, and besides, their range wasn't long enough to reach him from here. Short of battling her way through a horde of Silver-chomping zombies to go and ask him in person, Kulika didn't have any way to find out what his orders were, so she was stuck following his last one: wait for the zombies to go away.

That wasn't going to happen anytime soon.

It was hard not to consider her options. She had his ship. She had his covenant book, in the desk in his cabin. Most importantly, she had Quick and her friends, and they were safe. If she sailed away right now, what was Bartholomew going to do about it?

It was a risk, though, because with Bartholomew, who knew? Which meant it wasn't a decision she could make on her own.

'Mind the deck, Wolfs,' she said. 'I've got some thinking to do.' Then she headed down to the gun deck to speak to Quick and her friends.

They were lounging around in the hammocks, looking mournfully out of the gun ports. Kulika counted them up and found one missing.

'Where's Phinchas?' she asked.

'He said he'd be back,' said Evita. 'Then he ran off into the horde. Told us to drive back here and not to wait for him.'

'He ran into the zombies?' Kulika asked, horrified. She'd just assumed that Phinchas had come aboard with the others. In the chaos of their launch, she hadn't noticed that he wasn't there. 'When? Why?'

'On the road, about a mile out from the mansion.' Evita shrugged. 'He didn't say why. We thought maybe he had orders.'

'Not from me,' Kulika said.

On the other side of the gun deck, Xiaoyu was biting her lip and looking out at the river. With that many zombies in the water, Kulika thought she was right to be worried, but it turned out that wasn't the source of her misery.

'It's my fault,' Xiaoyu muttered. 'All of it. If I hadn't opened the blood cellar—'

'*You* opened the blood cellar?' Kulika asked, looking at Quick.

'You thought it was me?' Quick asked.

'Well, yeah. You have to admit, it fits your M.O.'

'Which I copied,' said Xiaoyu mournfully.

'You were trying to save them,' said Quick.

'But instead I doomed them all, and now Phinchas is gone…' Xiaoyu trailed off as her gaze wandered back out of the gunport.

'And I'm down one more sailor,' Kulika said to herself.

Which made the plan she had been contemplating far more intimidating. Following the current down the Cooper was one thing, but crossing the Atlantic in a Golden Age-era pirate ship? For a journey like that, you wanted safe hands on deck.

Without Phinchas, it would be harder to convince Wolfrie,

too. But maybe not impossible.

'What if we left?' Kulika asked.

'Left?' asked Quick.

'Just went,' said Kulika. 'What if we just sailed this ship away, left Bartholomew behind us, and never came back.'

'Is that even possible?' said Dr Ross. 'Won't it hurt you? Physically, I mean?'

'And won't the rest of the crew come after us to enforce Bartholomew's covenant?' Xiaoyu asked.

'Half of them are on this ship already,' Quick pointed out.

'Less than a quarter,' Kulika corrected her. 'But I think the others are going to be busy for a while cleaning up the mess the zombies are making back at the mansion. Maybe for a *long* while.'

'Bartholomew got his supernatural revelation,' Dr Ross commented wryly. 'Just not the one he was planning.'

'Exactly,' said Kulika. 'I don't think we're going to get a better opportunity to run. We could try, if you want.' She was asking them all, but she was looking at Quick. Her reply was the only one that really mattered.

'Do *you* want?' Quick asked.

In truth, Kulika wasn't sure. Everything she felt for Quick, everything she'd ever felt for Bartholomew, it was all mixed up in a pot of emotions she was struggling to sift. But that was what Bartholomew and his blood did to you, wasn't it? The best Kulika could do was cling to the certainty she'd had when she came back to South Carolina in the first place: she'd never wanted to return to Bartholomew, or to his mansion, and she'd only signed his covenant under duress, for Quick's sake. There had been a reason for that, whatever she was feeling now.

'So your head isn't hurting?' Evita asked her.

'No,' Kulika replied, with some surprise.

'Mine neither,' Evita replied, but she didn't look happy about it. 'We must be miles from the mansion by now. Our heads should be hurting.'

'Maybe Bartholomew died in the fire,' Wolfrie said, coming to join them below decks.

'Who's at the helm?' Kulika asked.

'Don't worry,' Wolfrie said, slumping into a nearby hammock. 'Bellamy's got it.'

Of all the crew from the old days, Bellamy was the one Kulika would have trusted least with the helm, but given the choice between him and Monty or his friends, she couldn't deny that Bellamy was the best option.

'You're thinking of sailing away, then?' Wolfrie asked. His hearing was sharp enough that he'd probably picked up their conversation from up on deck and decided to join them.

'Thinking about it, if we can get clear of Bartholomew.'

'I still think we should have killed him,' Wolfrie said.

Kulika glanced at Evita, remembering Wolfrie's plan. 'It wouldn't have worked.'

'It would have been better, though.'

'I don't know about that,' said Evita.

'You've changed your tune since this morning,' Quick pointed out. 'You kept telling me how dangerous he was, how he's killed so many people, how he deserves to die.'

'Well, a lot's happened since this morning,' Evita replied, a little too defensively.

'Then what do you think we should have done?' Quick asked.

'It's not just the fact that he kills people,' Xiaoyu interrupted. 'You know that, right? The point is that he *controls* people. The doc was just talking about this,' she added.

'I was,' Dr Ross murmured, glancing at the covenant mark

that stained Quick's palm. 'But it's academic now. There's no way to kill Bartholomew.'

'Right,' Kulika agreed. 'The only thing that might actually have killed him is the doctor's formula.'

'Not if he's from the Primus's – Solomon's, I mean – bloodline,' said Dr Ross. 'And I suspect he is. The formula wouldn't work on him. The only thing that would be strong enough to kill him would be the formula combined with Dr Jahan Khalyed's blood, which we don't have. I had hoped that Evita's blood would be a substitute, but…' Dr Ross smiled ruefully.

Kulika wondered if, like her, she was thinking about the baron and his impending death, which they had both been banking on Evita's blood to prevent. He had no hope now.

'Ancient history,' Dr Ross explained to the others. 'I tested a sample of Evita's blood that Bayly gave us. It wasn't a match to Jahan's. End of story. No point worrying about it now.'

'What are you talking about?' Evita said, confused. 'Bayly never took a sample of my blood.'

'While you were out of it, in the box,' Kulika explained.

'I was *never* out of it,' Evita insisted. 'I might have been weak and practically dead from blood loss, but I was conscious the entire time. I remember every single second of being stuck in that box. Believe me, I would have remembered if it had been opened, even for a second.'

'Then whose blood did I test?' Dr Ross asked, locking eyes with Kulika.

A long-dead hope started back to life in Kulika's chest. If they'd tested the wrong blood, then there was still a possibility that Evita's blood carried the same traits as Jahan's, and if it did…

They could save Baron Drake.

But Bayly. He'd *lied* to her. After all they'd been through together, after all she'd risked to wriggle him out of the covenant breach *he'd* created…

If he wasn't half-dead already, Kulika would have killed him herself.

'Whatever,' Evita said dismissively. 'It's done. We left Bartholomew behind. My blood doesn't matter now.'

Dr Ross glanced at Kulika as they shared the same silent thought: *it matters to Jack and the baron.*

'Yet somehow you're unhappy about leaving,' Quick was saying.

'Because it should hurt,' Evita said softly, 'like it did when we tried to leave the mansion this evening. But it doesn't hurt. Not at all.'

'Well, hopefully the zombies have killed him,' said Wolfrie.

'Unlikely,' Kulika replied.

'Dead or alive, they're welcome to him,' said Wolfrie. 'If you want to feel bad about anyone, then feel bad about Digs.'

'I will not,' said Kulika.

'Nor me,' said Evita pointedly.

'He was trying to kill us,' Kulika pointed out.

'But did he really deserve to die?' said Wolfrie. 'Bayly's the one who put him in that box. Who knows what that does to a mind. That much isolation…'

'Then all we did was put him out of his misery, right?' Kulika asked.

'But—'

'Wolfrie,' Kulika said. 'I know the two of you were close, but he deserved what he got. He even deserved being put in the damn box in the first place. You know that as well as I do.'

'Why?' asked Quick. 'What did he do?'

Wolfrie shrugged his rounded shoulders, then sighed and said, 'He was already old when Bayly locked him away over three hundred years ago. There isn't a person on this earth upwards of a hundred years old who hasn't done something they deserved to die for, me included.'

'And me,' Kulika said quietly. 'The longer you live, the more time you have to make an unforgivable choice.'

God knew she'd made enough of those.

'So let's hope this isn't one of them,' Wolfrie said.

'We're decided, then?' Dr Ross asked. 'We sail away?'

'We do it by the code,' Kulika corrected her. 'We take a vote, and if the crew's decided – the *new* crew – then we sail away, up along the coast if we can find a port that's safe, or all the way back to Britain if we have to. Agreed?'

'Agreed,' the others chorused.

Kulika looked at Dr Ross, who nodded back. If Evita's blood could do what they needed it to do, then they would get the cure to the baron as fast as they could, by hell or high water.

The vote didn't take long. Kulika and Wolfrie gathered everyone on deck, Silver and human, and asked for a show of hands from those who wanted to return to the mansion, to Bartholomew. The only taker was Monty.

Kulika let Quick push him off the side of the ship into the river, then told him to walk back on his own. Quick's evil grin as he splashed into the water was an image Kulika would cherish for the rest of her days.

20

UP AT THE front of the ship, with the midnight breeze pulling the hair back from her face, Quick was trying to forget everything that had happened today, if only for a moment.

Unfortunately, her mind didn't want to cooperate. It didn't help that the zombies were still following them through the water, grabbing onto the ship at the waterline and riding with it for a short distance before the current pulled them spinning away. Another would take the place of each that spun off almost immediately, so it seemed from above as though the ship was being carried down the river on the shoulders of a thousand night-shrouded wraiths.

This was not how Quick had thought her day would end. This morning, she'd been hopeful that they'd get out of the mansion and away from the crew for good. But then there had been Digs, and Evita's injuries, and from then on it had been a non-stop ride. She was finding, though, that she could tolerate the crew better without Monty and Bartholomew in it.

'Regrets?' Penny asked, coming to join her at what Quick was seventy-percent certain was the prow, though she wasn't brave enough to use the word. She had learned fast that Kulika and her pirates were twitchy about terminology.

'About a hundred of them,' Quick said.

'Anything you can do about them now?'

'Nope,' Quick replied.

'Then I wouldn't worry if I were you,' Penny said lightly, but it seemed like she was talking to herself more than she was talking to Quick.

They stood side by side for a few minutes in silence, watching the water and listening to the shouts in the rigging above and behind them. Kulika's voice rang out the clearest, strong and commanding as she managed the crew. That was Quick's only actionable regret, she realised: Kulika.

'Has anyone checked on Aloysius?' Quick asked.

'Who?' said Penny.

'The historian guy,' she explained. 'The one Bartholomew was keeping tied up in his cabin.'

Penny just gave her a blank look, so she said, 'Never mind. I'll go,' and went to check on the man herself.

Quick made her way down to the deck by the light of the ship's lanterns, watching her feet so she didn't trip over anything. The layout was so unfamiliar and the rocking motion so unbalancing that she often found herself bumping into railings and grasping for ropes that weren't there. Compared with the agile Silver in the rigging, she felt like a clumsy ox. Perhaps that grace would come with time, as she learned to control her powers and listen to her senses. She was a natural fighter, it seemed, but not a natural sailor.

So intent was she on her feet that she didn't notice she had company until she reached the doors leading into the captain's cabin. Kulika moved so silently that it was only her scent that tipped Quick off.

'Could we talk?' Kulika asked. Her gaze was shifting, her

focus moving from Quick's hair, to over her shoulder, to away into the darkness of the night. She wouldn't look Quick in the eye.

That didn't feel like a good sign.

'Sure,' Quick said, trying to calm the anxiety building in her stomach.

Dr Ross had told her the silvering was reversing. Was that what Kulika was about to confess to her? That she didn't love her anymore, and that this thing between them was over before it had even begun? Because Quick wasn't sure she'd be able to bear that. It was far from over for her. She could feel the electricity between them in the anticipatory tingle of her fingertips as they ached to reach out and grasp the bare skin of Kulika's shoulders. Her yearning was there in the dryness that suddenly invaded her mouth, making the urge to lick her lips irresistible. And surely that yearning was reflected back to her in the way Kulika's gaze followed her tongue as she licked?

But Quick couldn't see the silver that Kulika was hiding in her eyes, so she had no way of knowing. She'd have to do this the hard way, and ask.

'I was just going to check on Aloysius,' Quick said. 'That is, unless you've already—'

'No,' Kulika replied. 'I'd forgotten about him, honestly.'

'Maybe we could go together?' Quick asked, holding the door open.

Kulika took a deep breath, as though she were preparing herself for a distasteful task, then stepped through the door and into what had until recently been Bartholomew's cabin. Like a pirate to the gallows, Quick followed reluctantly behind.

To Kulika, Bartholomew's cabin felt like a museum without him in it. It was so familiar from their years at sea together that while he had inhabited this replica, she'd felt as though no time had passed since the Golden Age. Now, void of the character that held these antique pieces together, she could finally see it for what it was: a relic of a bygone era. There might as well have been cobwebs hanging from the ceiling.

'He's not here,' Quick said.

For a moment, the threads got crossed in Kulika's mind and she thought Quick was talking about Bartholomew, then she saw the discarded ropes tossed by the foot of the bed and remembered they were supposed to be looking for Aloysius. That wasn't why Kulika had followed Quick here, though.

'I thought maybe we should talk,' Kulika said. She had to do this fast, because if she put it off then it was just going to keep building and building like an avalanche until she couldn't hold it back anymore, and then it would all come out wrong.

'Okay,' Quick said, turning to face her. 'About the silvering?'

Kulika froze.

'Dr Ross said it was reversing,' Quick added.

Of course she did. Kulika should have guessed that the doctor would stick her oar in. Maybe that was a good thing. If Quick already knew what was happening, Kulika could just nod and leave. It would be easier that way.

'Then you know,' she said, heading for the door. 'That was all I wanted to talk about, really.'

'Hey, wait,' said Quick, rushing after her. 'We haven't actually *talked* at all, though. You've just confirmed what I already knew.'

'So we're done,' Kulika said, puzzled. 'Aren't we?'

'*Are* we?' Quick asked, stepping forward until she was close enough for Kulika to reach out and touch.

She didn't, though. She couldn't let herself do that. It

wasn't fair, not now that all of this was going away. Maybe it had never been fair, given the circumstances of Quick's turning, and all the liberties that Kulika had taken since. With her position, she should never have touched Quick in the first place. Looking back now, all she could hear was Bartholomew's voice in her head, a guilty reminder of everything she never should have done.

We don't ask, we take.

Well, Kulika had taken. Now she could only apologise for it.

'I'm sorry,' Kulika said. 'For everything.'

'I don't want your apologies,' Quick said irritably. 'I want the truth. I want to know how you *feel*. You're acting as though this thing between us is over, but it doesn't feel over, not to me.'

'Doesn't it?' Kulika asked, because to her it felt as though Quick was still slipping through her fingers like sand through an hourglass.

'If you tell me I've had all I'm ever going to get of you, then fine,' Quick said, 'I'll take it on the chin and walk away, but that's not what I want. If it's not what you want either, then maybe we can find a way to reverse the reversing, but right now I have no idea how you feel about any of this.' Quick took one step closer until she was looking right up into Kulika's eyes. 'You said you wanted to talk, so talk to me. Please.'

Kulika broke, like a wave against the rocks.

'I love you,' she whispered, suddenly holding back tears that seemed to have sprung from nowhere. 'I do, or I did. But—'

Then the pain ripped through her, starting at her stomach and tearing out through her veins so it felt like her body was trying to turn itself inside out. She doubled over, breathing through her screams. When the pain subsided enough for her to be conscious of her surroundings again, she found herself kneeling on the floor in Quick's arms, holding her head and wincing.

'What was that?' Quick asked, fear written all over her face.

'The blood and the bond,' Kulika gasped, still getting her breath back.

'Blood?'

'I drank Bartholomew's blood when I made my bargain with him,' Kulika admitted. 'And again today. The doc says it's messing with the bond.'

'Which bargain?' Quick asked.

'In the book in his desk drawer,' Kulika said. 'Get it.' Then she slumped back against the bulkhead as Quick crossed the cabin to the stern.

Once Quick had taken the covenant book from the drawer, she brought it back to sit beside Kulika on the floor.

'Me, and Evita, and Xiaoyu,' Quick murmured as she found the right page and read.

'Good deal, right?' Kulika replied with a wry laugh, but she was distracted by the scent of Quick's blood spilling from the book. She turned the page in Quick's unresisting hands to find Quick's own bargain spelled out in blood on the next spread: her covenant in return for Bartholomew's blood to heal to Evita.

'Not such a good deal,' Quick said bitterly.

'We're leaving him behind us,' Kulika said, then she snatched the book from Quick's hands and tossed it across the room. 'We'll burn it.'

'And these?' Quick took Kulika's tattooed hand in her own, laying them both across her lap palm up, so the matching brands looked like a pair of dark eyes holding the two of them in their gaze.

'We'll burn them, too,' Kulika whispered, then she covered Quick's tattoo with her own, clasping them together as she clasped Quick's hand.

But Kulika knew she couldn't burn Bartholomew's blood out of her veins as easily as she could burn his mark off her skin. The pain wasn't going away, it was just coming in smaller waves. It swirled between the two of them, threatening to drag Kulika into its undertow.

'I don't know if I'll ever be able to get free of him,' Kulika said softly. 'However far we sail, whatever the world becomes. He's part of me.'

'And me,' Quick replied, squeezing Kulika's hand. 'His blood is in me too, even if it's only a drop.'

'His voice is in my head.'

'For now. You don't have to listen to it if you don't want to.'

Was that true, Kulika wondered? Was Quick a choice she'd ever be allowed to make on her own, without him watching over her shoulder and whispering in her ear?

Then she turned to look at Quick and saw exactly how much Bartholomew had stolen from her.

'Your eyes,' she said.

'Hmm?' Quick asked. She was looking at Kulika in a thoughtful way that made Kulika want to rip all her clothes off, but her eyes…

'Your eyes are silver,' Kulika said in a hollow voice.

'What?'

Quick pushed away from the bulkhead and up to her feet, then found a hand mirror on Bartholomew's bedside table and looked at her eyes. Kulika knew what she'd be seeing: the silver that traced the blood vessels in her eyes had now extended into the rich green of her irises, radiating towards her pupils so they looked like they were surrounded by emerald feathers, highlighted in platinum.

'But that's not possible,' Quick said, turning to Kulika in shock. 'Dr Ross told me how it works: when you silver for someone who's already silvered for you, the silver turns gold, in your eyes and in the eyes of the person you love. Bound in silver, sealed in gold. That's what the doctor said. Requited love is supposed to be golden, not silver.'

'Maybe it's not me you've silvered for,' Kulika said bleakly as the horror of that possibility ran through her like a chill.

'Don't be ridiculous,' Quick said dismissively. She looked at Kulika for a moment, then crouched down next to her on the floor and said, 'Show me your silver.'

'I love *you*,' Kulika insisted.

Which set off another wave of excruciating pain that she had to ride until it was over. When she blinked back to awareness this time, she was lying on the floor with Quick leaning over her. Apparently she'd lost control of her silver during that episode, because the first thing Quick said was, 'It's gone.' She looked as though she was going to cry. 'The silver isn't in your irises anymore, just the whites of your eyes.'

Quick grabbed the mirror again and passed it to Kulika so she could see for herself, but Kulika pushed it away. She believed Quick. She didn't want to see it for herself. She didn't need to; she could feel the emptiness in her chest that had been left behind by Bartholomew's vindictive jealousy.

'I should have killed him,' she said, but the words had no force. Apparently, with this much of Bartholomew's blood in her, she couldn't even hate him properly.

She looked at Quick hopelessly, tracing the shimmer of silver in her irises with her gaze. How unfair. It was the promise of a perfect ending that might have been fulfilled, if only Bartholomew hadn't got in the way. It had been so nearly within her grasp.

How terribly fucking unfair.

'This doesn't mean it has to be the end, does it?' Quick asked.

'I don't know,' Kulika replied.

She didn't know what it meant. She didn't know what any of it meant, because she'd never seen this happen before. Never even heard of it happening before. It shouldn't be possible to reverse a bond. It shouldn't be possible for one Silver to impose their will on another just by infecting them with their blood. It shouldn't be possible for a bond like Kulika and Quick's to be broken.

And yet.

'Kulika?' Wolfrie called from the deck.

'Yeah?' Kulika called back. She was too deflated to move.

'Can you come out here?'

'Why?' she groaned, not relishing the prospect of returning to teach Seafaring 101.

But then Wolfrie called back with, 'I think we've found the historian.'

<h1 style="text-align:center">21</h1>

KULIKA FOLLOWED WOLFRIE down to the bottom deck of the ship with Quick trailing along behind. Part of her wished that Quick had stayed up top in the captain's cabin. After everything that had just happened, she didn't know how to look Quick in the eye and not see self-reproach written in the silver threading through her irises.

Kulika should never have bargained with Bartholomew. She knew him well enough to know that he would turn every deal to his own overwhelming profit, even when it was Kulika setting the terms. Now, she couldn't help but wonder if he'd known exactly what his blood would do to her. He'd experimented with it in every other way, she was sure, but using it to break a Silver bond? It felt calculated and cruel enough to be deliberate, but silvering was so rare that she couldn't imagine he'd ever had the opportunity to test it before.

It was too late to ask him now.

They found Aloysius bundled up in a chest in the gun magazine room, behind the galley.

'Is he alive?' Quick asked.

'Yes,' said Kulika. She could hear his pulse, strong and

regular. 'Drugged, probably. Let's get him out. Can you get Dr Ross, please?'

Kulika hadn't addressed this request to either of them in particular, but it was Quick who said, 'I'll go.'

When she returned with the doctor, Kulika and Wolfrie had Aloysius laid out on the floor. There was a conspicuous needle mark in his arm.

'Dr Ross,' Kulika said.

'It's probably time you all started calling me Tabitha,' she replied with a grim smile.

'Tabitha, then. Can you do anything for him?'

'Maybe,' she said, examining the needle mark in his arm. 'If the infirmary is stocked with any supplies from this century.'

'It's one level up, at the stern,' said Kulika. 'The cabin with the broken window. You can't miss it.'

'Broken window?' the doctor said uncertainly.

'It's how Digs got in,' Wolfrie explained.

'I guess we'd better patch it up before we head out into the Atlantic,' Kulika said, wondering how many other things they'd have to patch up on the journey.

This ship had never been designed to go to sea, and most of the people who'd built it had never made a ship like this before in their lives. Maybe they'd be better off stopping at the harbour for a more modern vessel, but that would delay them, and Kulika didn't want to delay even for a moment. Delay meant more exposure, more vicious zombies to fight through, and more chance that Bartholomew would come after them.

Kulika and Wolfrie knew what they were doing, and that would have to be enough. They could manage the risk, just until they reached the next port up the coast.

'I'll find some tools and meet you in the infirmary,'

Wolfrie said to the doctor.

'I'll help you get him upstairs,' Quick offered.

'Then I'll go and make sure we're sailing in the right direction,' said Kulika.

She hadn't even reached the main deck before Wolfrie called her name again.

'Kulika?'

'Yeah?'

'Can you come here, please?'

It was the "please" that told her something was wrong. Pirates didn't have much time for politeness. If you hesitated on board, whether in battle or when navigating in a storm, people died and ships sank. You didn't ask nicely when a job needed doing, you just demanded what was required and left courtesy to those who could afford it. A habit like that crept into your everyday way of speaking, and your way of doing, until it became an unshakeable characteristic.

Pirates didn't say please.

That's why, when she heard that word, Kulika ran to the infirmary. She found Wolfrie, Quick and Dr Ross staring at the patient's bunk. It wasn't occupied by Bayly or Enzo, who seemed to be missing, or by Aloysius, who'd been abandoned on the floor at their feet, but rather by Evita – and Bartholomew, who was sitting calmly on the bed next to her, wiping blood from his face with a wet cloth. There was blood all over him, the majority of which was flowing from scrapes on his shoulders, perhaps caused as he'd climbed in through the broken window. His arms were pockmarked with bite marks that had left bloody rosettes over his white shirt. There was a gaping wound over his heart that looked like it had been dug out with nails and teeth, and there were a couple of bites on his face, too, ripped through his cheeks so he bore more than a passing resemblance to the creature they had once called Digs. If this was how he looked *after* he'd healed, Kulika didn't want to imagine how bad the wounds had been when they'd first been inflicted.

'My Second,' he said to her.

It was a statement of possession, and it shivered through Kulika in the worst possible way.

You're an empty thing without me.

She was an emptier thing with him. She hadn't realised until this moment just how free she'd felt when she thought he'd no longer had any claim on her.

But the lack of pain she'd felt at their separation made sense now. She hadn't hurt when she'd left the mansion, despite the amount of Bartholomew's blood she'd drunk, because he hadn't been *at* the mansion. He'd been right here all along, stowed away on the *Primus's Fortune* with the other stragglers. If Kulika hadn't been so distracted by her attempts to command a frigate for the first time in three centuries, and her attempts to salvage her relationship with Quick, she might have noticed his scent on board. Now that it was in her nostrils, it was stuck in there like the cloying odour of mould, impossible to ignore.

And impossible to cure.

He was in her head, and in her veins, and she couldn't raise a hand against him, however hard she tried. She was powerless against Bartholomew Roberts.

Just as he'd always wanted her to be.

Quick had never cared that she couldn't hide her silver, not until the moment that Bartholomew's gaze landed on her. The way he smiled when he saw her newly-silvered eyes made her stomach turn.

'Show me your silver,' he said to Kulika.

Without a word, and apparently helpless to resist, Kulika did exactly as he asked.

Bartholomew's smile twitched a fraction wider.

'Here we all are, then,' he said, curling one hand around Evita's waist while he tucked her hair over her shoulder with the other, baring her neck. The gesture felt like a threat, one that gave Quick pause. Meanwhile, Evita just sat placidly, appearing perfectly content to let herself be held and stroked by the man who, only this morning, she'd been champing at the bit to murder.

There was only one explanation Quick could come up with: Bartholomew's blood. Maybe Dr Ross was right. Maybe there was something in that. He hadn't just wanted Quick to sign the covenant, he'd wanted his blood inside Evita, so he could control her like he was doing now. Like he was probably controlling Kulika, too.

'You've already charted our journey?' Bartholomew said to Kulika.

'I've started, Primus,' she replied, as though she'd expected him to be joining them all along.

For a moment, Quick wondered if that was the truth of the situation, but she wasn't imagining the way Kulika was clenching her jaw and fisting her hands. She could feel her tension, too, like someone was strumming at the tether that connected her to Kulika through her new bond.

'Then perhaps we should reconvene in my cabin, to consult the maps,' Bartholomew suggested. 'I assume it's back to Britain?'

'Unless we can find safe harbour along the coast,' Kulika said, the words apparently falling uncontrollably from her mouth.

'Kulika,' Wolfrie said, looking at her in shock. 'You're not really going to just step aside and go along with—'

'There's no safe harbour in North America,' Bartholomew said bluntly, ignoring Wolfrie entirely. 'The zombies are spreading too fast.'

'And just how much of that did you design?' Dr Ross asked. She was crouched anxiously on the floor beside Aloysius, who was finally starting to come around. 'Kulika said you had hours in that wine cellar with Digs and the zombies. You had plenty of time to study them.'

Bartholomew shrugged the shoulder that wasn't pressed up against Evita. 'I found that Digs liked the taste of my blood.'

'You knew he'd come after us,' Quick breathed.

'I had expected he would do it sooner, before you left the property at all. The zombies were a collateral effect that, I admit, I could have done without. I chained them to the wall, but…' He sighed. 'I'd owned that mansion for three hundred years, you know,' he added mournfully. 'By the end of the night, it'll be ash.'

'Do you really expect us to feel bad for you?' Quick sneered.

'Why should you?' he asked jovially. 'I have everything I want right here: my crew, my ship, my Second.'

He turned to Evita, pushing her hair behind her ear.

Quick could imagine what he wanted from her best friend, and she didn't like it at all. Something flared in Evita's eyes then, and Quick wondered if perhaps she wasn't as subjugated as she appeared. In the next second, Evita had snatched Bartholomew's hand away from her face and swung a punch at him, which he caught in his palm with infuriating ease.

With that, the spell broke. Up until now, Bartholomew had been able to pretend that everything was as he wanted it, but now even he couldn't deny that the cracks were beginning to show.

'I thought I'd found something in you, something that I'd

never even thought to look for,' Bartholomew said to Evita, his top lip twisting into a grimace as he held her fists in his hands.

'Do you love her?' Wolfrie asked abruptly. He was weighing the box of tools he held in his hand like he meant to do something with them. Quick didn't like the way his gaze was fixing on Evita.

'Is that what you think?' Bartholomew asked him, with a harsh bark of laughter. 'You think I've silvered for a whelp, like my Second has? Well, I'm afraid I have to disappoint you. I won't be that easy to kill.'

The whites of Bartholomew's eyes flashed silver for a moment, but there was nothing in his irises except stormy grey. Wolfrie deflated, looking hopelessly at Kulika, who was doing nothing at all.

In the meantime, Bartholomew had turned back to Evita. 'I thought I'd found a *connection*,' he said angrily to her.

'You had,' Evita shot back with equal vitriol. 'That's the really sad thing, you know? I could have loved you. Maybe you could even have loved me, but you never gave us a chance to find out.'

Bartholomew laughed. 'You forgot me,' he said. His tone was disdainful, but Quick didn't think she was imagining the pain she heard in it too.

'When I lost my memory, I didn't choose to forget you,' Evita replied. 'That wasn't in my control. You did, though. You're the one who chose to forget me. To forget *us*.'

Bartholomew's expression switched from anger to pain, and back again. The cracks broke wide open, irreparable and unfathomable. He hurled Evita to the floor and stood from the bunk in a blood-soaked rage, towering over her as he yelled, 'I *made* you! I made all of you,' he added, looking first at Kulika, then at Quick, before turning back to Evita.

It was true: Kulika and Evita had both been turned by Bartholomew himself. Quick had been turned by Kulika. All three of them shared his blood, and the yoke that went along with it. He controlled them all.

'A little respect wouldn't go amiss,' he was saying to Evita. 'Have you forgotten who I am? I am your Primus, and the captain of this ship.' He looked at Dr Ross and Aloysius, then at Wolfrie, saying, 'If you're on this ship, then you're part of my crew, and my crew will enforce my word. If you prefer to leave, then the zombies are welcome to you.'

'Your crew are all back at the mansion,' Wolfrie pointed out. 'What you have here is a handful of deserters and a hold full of frightened humans, none of whom belong to you.'

'Don't they?' Bartholomew asked, pacing closer. 'My Second controls this ship, does she not?'

Wolfrie tipped his head in evasive acknowledgement.

'Then she does so on my behalf. Isn't that right, Kulika?'

Kulika said, 'I...'

But that was all she said.

Quick wanted her to argue. She'd *seen* Kulika argue with Bartholomew, in bright blazes of emotion, but now she was subdued, weighed down by the poison of his blood in her veins. Evita was the same: she might have mustered up enough strength to swing at Bartholomew once, but she wasn't trying to repeat it now. Instead, she just lay on the floor, staring up at him with a look of painful frustration that Quick couldn't bear. The two most powerful women in her life, the two women she loved, reduced to this.

'You understand, don't you, Dr Ross?' Bartholomew asked the doctor. 'You know what would happen if you left this ship right now.'

'The zombies are infecting every human in North America,' she replied softly. 'When they do, there'll be nothing left for us to drink.'

'Exactly. I control the blood supply on this ship, and with it I control the rest of you. It's me, or a long, painful death.'

'One and the same,' Quick spat.

Unlike them, she had never been under his spell. She might share Bartholomew's blood, but she'd been turned by Kulika, at one remove from him. Her bloodline was diluted, and she'd drunk a lot less of his blood recently than the other two had.

'Do you really want to test me, Patience?' Bartholomew asked, almost playfully. 'You're not the only one who signed my covenant.'

He grabbed Kulika's hand, then drove his fingernail into the black spot in the centre of her palm and twisted it. She didn't scream, but her lips went white. Her pain was so palpable that Quick was sure she felt it in the mark on her own scarred palm.

'With your silvering, I have you as surely as I have her,' Bartholomew whispered, then he tossed Kulika's hand away and said, 'Now set course for—'

Quick didn't recall moving. All she recalled was a simple chain of thoughts: She was strong. She was fast. If the two people she loved most in the world weren't able to save themselves, then she would do it for them.

Her hand slipped into her pocket and brought up the vial-filled syringe, flipped off the cap, then plunged it into the messy open wound that had been gouged over Bartholomew's heart.

He looked down first in surprise, then in irritation.

'My blood is not so weak as all that,' he said, laughing as he plucked the vial easily from Quick's fingers and tossed it away.

Dr Ross had been right, then: Bartholomew's veins really

did flow with the blood of Primus Solomon. If they didn't, he'd be dead right now. Instead, he was pinning Quick to the infirmary wall by her throat, leaving her feet to kick uselessly in the air.

'Foolish, Patience,' he said. 'Have you not realised that you're useless to me now that my Second's silvering has reversed? I can kill you with no consequences to her at all. Maybe she'll mourn you, for a day or two,' he said, leaning in closer so Quick could feel his breath on her cheek and smell the rancid putrescence of his open wounds. 'But I doubt it.'

Quick struggled and kicked, but Bartholomew was too strong for her. She looked at Kulika over his shoulder, searching desperately for help, but Kulika wouldn't meet her gaze. Instead, her eyes were fixed on the floor as Bartholomew's mouth lowered towards Quick's neck.

Kulika wasn't going to do a thing about this, Quick realised. After fighting to protect Quick from Digs, and even after the declaration of love she'd made in the captain's cabin mere minutes before, Kulika was just going to stand there and do nothing while Bartholomew tore Quick's throat out. Bartholomew controlled Kulika, and Evita, and Quick along with them.

Quick was going to die waiting to be saved by a woman who was no more capable of saving her from Bartholomew than she was of saving herself.

They'd never stood a chance.

Or so Quick had thought, but when she looked again, Kulika was no longer on the other side of the infirmary. Instead, she was standing right next to Quick, with Evita's wrist held tightly in her hand. In the blink of an eye, she took a knife from her pocket and used it to slice open Evita's palm, then slammed it onto the ugly gash where Quick had plunged the vial into Bartholomew's chest.

Bartholomew looked at Kulika, then down at Evita's hand as she withdrew it hastily, then back at Kulika.

'What's that supposed to achieve?' he asked derisively.

'An end to this,' Kulika whispered. 'I'm sorry, Bartholomew. I really am.'

'Sorry?' he laughed. 'For what, exactly?'

Then something changed.

Bartholomew looked down at his seeping chest in horror. 'What is this, Kulika?' he asked. 'Mutiny? Again?'

'I may have your blood,' Kulika said to him softly. 'But Quick still has my heart.'

Bartholomew threw Quick aside, slamming her head against the wall and crumpling her into a heap on the floor. It wasn't until she gathered her wits back together and looked up at him, blinking, that she realised what Kulika had done. Against all the odds, Evita had inherited Jahan Khalyed's immunity to the formula. By adding Evita's blood to the concoction that Quick had already injected into his chest, Kulika had created a poison that even Bartholomew couldn't overcome.

He was stepping back towards the bed now, throwing a wild punch at Kulika as he went, but she ducked it easily. He stumbled to his knees, following the force of his swing to the ground.

Quick could feel the heat, then. Bartholomew stared down in disbelief at the spot on his chest where the syringe and Evita's palm had found their mark, watching as the blood within the wound began to glow. Soon, the glow was visible through the surrounding skin, blending from red to orange to yellow to white hot as it burned the clothes from his body. Dark cracks blossomed out from it like black rot through infected veins, spreading down his arms and up his neck until they crossed his chin to reach for his lips.

He looked up. His gaze found Evita's.

'I knew you'd be the death of me,' he whispered with a smile.

Then the flames took him. All that was left when it was over was the copper token he'd worn at his neck, tinkling onto the charred surface of the deck.

22

AS THE SHIP sailed past White Point Gardens in the early hours of the morning, a small motorised dinghy pushed off from the tip of the Battery in Charleston Harbour and started heading in their direction. There were four people on board: two adults, and two children. Xiaoyu's children, as it turned out, plus her former husband, and Phinchas.

'Found them in the attic,' Phinchas said as he passed the children up the rope ladder and into their mother's arms.

They all cried for a while after that. Kulika and the others left them to it, giving over the navigation room so they could have a space to be together as a family, after so long apart.

Phinchas went with them. Kulika wondered about that, until she saw Xiaoyu reach out and take his hand behind her back, where the rest of her family couldn't see it.

Maybe they would get their happy ending after all.

Kulika wasn't so sure about her own. It had been mere minutes since Bartholomew had been reduced to ash in the infirmary, and she was still shedding the influence of his blood like a snake shedding its skin. It was coming off messily, in dirty pieces that got stuck in her teeth, leaving too many parts of her raw and exposed.

He had been everything to her. He was nothing now, except another notch on her conscience that she would never quite shake.

She'd come up to the sterncastle for the air, though there was plenty of that on the ship. Perhaps what she'd really wanted was somewhere she could stand and see everything she was leaving behind her, to convince herself it was real. There was Charleston, disappearing into the night. There were the fires lighting the horizon, from the mansion and any number of other properties that had been set alight in the panic induced by the zombies. If Kulika looked down at the wake of the *Primus's Fortune* as it set out for the Atlantic, she could still see them bobbing in the water behind them. That didn't seem like a good omen.

Kulika didn't get to enjoy her solitude for long, which was just as well.

'Ms Yadav,' the man said, with all the grace of a proper Southern gentleman. 'I know we've already met, but we've not yet been properly introduced. Allow me to do the honours: Aloysius Truman, Chairman of the Charleston Historical Society, amateur historian, and your humble servant.' He bowed.

The man actually *bowed*.

'I was intending to write a history of Bartholomew Roberts,' he said, 'but perhaps, since his – *ahem* – unfortunate demise, I might write yours instead?'

Kulika looked down again at the zombies in their wake.

'Knock yourself out,' she replied. 'But if that's really what you want to do, then I suggest you do it fast.'

'I have some questions,' he said, pulling a notepad from his pocket with a gleam in his eye. 'If you could just—'

Evita came to join them then, giving Kulika a convenient excuse.

'Later, Aloysius,' she said.

The man bowed again, then left Kulika and Evita alone, but not before giving her the distinct impression that he would be back. Apparently, she had a fan now, and he would be sticking around.

'Thank you,' Evita said. 'For… you know.'

Kulika said nothing. She didn't want credit for any of it. She'd killed her sire and her captain. Where she came from, they had punishments enough to fit a crime like that.

ARTICLE VI. No boy or woman to be allowed amongst them.

ARTICLE VIII. None shall strike another on board the ship.

ARTICLE VII. He that shall desert the ship or his quarters in time of battle shall be punished by death or marooning.

But now the Articles of Bartholomew Roberts were just ash in the galley stove, along with his covenant book and all the blood trapped between its pages.

'Do you feel it too?' Evita asked her.

'Feel what?'

'Nothing.' Evita smiled, looking out over the dark water. 'No pain in your veins, no clamp on your tongue, no voice in your head except yours.'

'Yes.' Kulika smiled back. 'I feel it.'

Had Kulika ever truly *felt* a night breeze in the past three centuries, one that hadn't been muted by the armour she wore? The wind skittered across her skin with a chill that shocked and thrilled her, teasing her hair from her forehead like it wanted to play.

'Evita,' Dr Ross said, climbing the steps from the quarterdeck.

'Yes?' Evita replied, her eyes still fixed on the distant water.

'I want to test your blood,' the doctor said. 'Properly this time.'

'Is that really necessary?' Kulika asked, leaning back against the gunwale to face Dr Ross. 'Don't we have our answer?'

'Yes,' Dr Ross conceded, 'but I want to have Baron Drake's antidote ready by the time we get back home. It'll take a while, particularly with the limited resources on board, so I want to start right now.'

'But you think you'll be able to do it?' Kulika asked, pushing herself up straight.

'Yes,' the doctor replied with a hopeful smile. 'Now I just need you to get us back to him in time.'

'We're already too late, aren't we?' Kulika pointed out sadly, remembering the baron's desperation in their last phone calls.

'We don't know that. Give him and Jack some credit. They're more creative than you might think.'

'Let's hope so,' Kulika said, with not much hope at all.

Dr Ross remained buoyant, though. When Quick came to complete their quartet, the little doctor smiled widely and pulled her into her arms.

'I knew you could do it,' she said.

Quick smiled at Dr Ross, then came to stand next to Kulika at the railing. When she raised her eyes to Kulika's, they were glinting with gold.

Gold.

'Have you seen your—' Kulika began, breathlessly.

'I know,' Quick said with a smile. 'Will you show me yours?'

Kulika did, relaxing the control she held over the silver in her eyes as she stared at the gold in Quick's. But she could feel immediately that her own were no longer silver at all.

Where the silver had always shot back into her eyes with a pinch, the gold moved in a sluggish caress, coaxing Kulika to a joyful crescendo as she felt the colour circle her pupils in triumph.

There was no fogged glass between them now. Though Quick's colour had seemed dull only hours before, her hair was now a riot of sunset and sunrise, and her scent…

Frost-chilled pine trees in thick winter forests; sunshine breaking late over crocus-filled verges; summer heat baking yellow climbing roses; plums ripening beyond the constraints of their skins and spilling golden drops of sugar down their sides.

Quick's scent was all of these things at once, and none of them, her perfume kaleidoscoping through all the seasons, and rising joyfully as Kulika took her face in her hands. She pressed a kiss to Quick's lips, tentatively at first, but then Quick flicked her tongue and it was all that Kulika could do to stop herself from laying her down right there on the deck in front of their audience. Kulika kissed her like she meant it then, with intent and emotion, trying to convey with her actions the simple things that she found hard to put into words.

She loved Quick.

Quick loved her.

However many zombies were in the water, nothing could be wrong with the world as long as those two things remained true. And now that Bartholomew was gone, they would remain true, forever.

An hour before dawn, Bayly and Enzo woke up. The others were sitting on the main deck, drinking and planning, when they slunk upstairs from the officers' mess where Bartholomew had left them.

Quick was horrified.

'Wait! Hey, we're not letting him just run around on deck, are we?' she asked when she saw Bayly.

'Why not?' Kulika replied.

'Yeah,' said Wolfrie.

'Why not?' Phinchas finished.

'Because he's responsible for all this,' Quick said. She looked around at each of their confused faces in turn and didn't believe what she was seeing. 'He caused a zombie apocalypse! If he hadn't put Evita and Digs in that box together, then none of this would have happened.'

'But he's crew,' Wolfrie said simply.

'Plus,' said Penny, 'it was technically Bella who stole the formula from the lab and made the first super-zombie.'

'Though to be fair, she wouldn't have got her hands on that formula if Dr Ross had been paying attention,' said Brandon.

'Excuse *me*,' the doctor piped up. 'If you'd *all* been managing yourselves a little better, I wouldn't have had to. Besides, neither Kulika nor I would have come here in the first place if it wasn't for Baron Drake.'

'Who wouldn't have sent us if Jack Valentine hadn't gone and poisoned herself,' Kulika added.

'By accident,' said Dr Ross.

'But really, all of this was Bartholomew's fault,' Phinchas pointed out.

'He's dead, by the way,' Kulika added to Bayly, whose only reply was, 'Good.'

'Look,' said Quick, 'all of those things might be true, but he put my best friend in a box with a monster. I don't trust him.'

'Stand down, Impatience,' Evita said with a sigh. She was busy cleaning a knife as she prepared to excise the black mark from Quick's hand, again. 'Let the bastard be. He was a prisoner here as much as the rest of us were.'

'Seriously?' Quick looked across the deck to where Bayly was now lounging against the rigging with Enzo at his feet, as though he hadn't a care in the world. She turned back to Evita and asked, 'You're fine with this?'

'I'm fine.' Evita ran the knife blade through the flame of the lantern that hung beside her. 'It wasn't Bayly I was angry with.'

'But he put you in a box with a blood-starved vampire. He buried you and left you, for weeks. If Kulika hadn't come along and found you when she did, god knows how long you would've been stuck in—'

Evita whirled and let the knife fly, sending it right into Bayly's eye. Apparently she'd learned some new skills during her time at the mansion. Bayly sagged in the ropes, then fell face-first onto the deck.

'Hey!' Enzo yelled.

'He'll live,' Evita yelled back. 'Okay, now I'm fine,' she added as she turned back to Quick. 'I can't promise I'm not going to do that again from time to time, but I'm fine.'

Quick looked at Bayly's prostrate body, then squinted sceptically at Evita.

'Truly,' Evita said. 'I got it out of my system. I got *him* out of my system, and his blood with it.'

'Out of *all* of our systems,' Quick added. 'You sort of saved the day.'

'You and Kulika did, you mean. And let's not get carried away. We're still in the middle of a zombie apocalypse. Speaking of which, what happens if the zombies are in Britain by the time we arrive? If they really did contaminate the planes—'

'Then we'll deal with it then,' said Kulika calmly. 'For now, it's just us and the sea.'

Phinchas smiled and said, 'The way you always liked it, Captain.'

Kulika smiled back at him.

Quick was coming to learn that, on the water, *now* was all that mattered. Now, she had her best friend back, and if they both tried very hard, they could pretend she'd never been gone in the first place. Now, Bartholomew Roberts was nothing but a pirate who'd received less attention than the scale of his fleet warranted, just as he always had been. Now, Quick and Kulika had each other, as they always should have done. The in-between didn't matter, and neither did what was still to come.

On the water, they could live for now, and deal with tomorrow later.

Kulika finished plotting their course just before dawn. She took her place on the quarterdeck when she was done, and Quick came with her. Quick had come with her everywhere since the moment their bond had sealed into gold, and Kulika wasn't complaining about it. If she had her way, they'd never be parted again.

'Where to, Captain?' Wolfrie asked, his arm resting on the wheel.

'Into the sunrise,' she said, smiling at Quick.

Home.

'I'd better get below decks,' Quick laughed.

'Or you could stay here with me,' Kulika suggested, running her fingers into Quick's hair, then using that point of contact to send the healing power of their bond through Quick's body.

'You mean—'

'I think so,' Kulika said. 'As long as you keep contact with me, I can heal you before you even start to burn.'

'So we can watch the sunrise together?'

'Every morning, if you like.'

The sun broke over the horizon then, and Kulika settled her hand at the nape of Quick's neck, playing with the soft strands of hair there as they watched the dawning of their new world. Quick snuggled into her side, resting her cheek on Kulika's chest in the indentation below her shoulder that seemed to have been made to accommodate Quick, and no one else.

'Beautiful,' Quick murmured as she watched the sun rise.

'By the time we get home, you should be immune to it,' Kulika replied.

'How long will it take to get back to Britain?'

'Four weeks, if we're lucky. Eight if we're not.'

'That long?'

'This is a proper ship,' Kulika said, stroking the wood of the railing fondly. 'She doesn't have engines, or oars, or propellers. She rides the waves at the whims of the wind.'

Quick smiled, squinting a little as she turned towards the new sun. 'You get poetic about the sea.'

'I could get poetic about something else if you prefer,' Kulika offered in a whisper, stroking her fingers through Quick's flame-red hair. Then she leaned in and kissed her neck, savouring the frost and hedgerow flavour of her skin. Quick's scent kaleidoscoped as Kulika did so, singing through sharp citrus to winter spice, then ripening into something more enticing still. 'I can be very poetic, with my lips,' Kulika murmured against Quick's skin.

'Yes, please,' Quick breathed.

Well, why not? They'd seen enough of the sunrise for one morning, and they were pirates, weren't they? It was past time they started acting like it. For once in her life, Kulika had permission to take the things she wanted, and she wasn't going to let the opportunity go to waste.

Thrilling at every untethered step, Kulika took Quick down to the berth where they kept the rum, and showed her just how poetical – and piratical – she could be.

If you enjoyed *Quick and the Dead*, why not read *Dead Road*? They're serialised sequel episodes to the *QuickSilver* series, following a load of new characters as they navigate the zombie apocalypse.

***

Join my Readers' Club and receive a FREE short story

www.josiejaffrey.com/subscribe

***

Please leave a review!

If you enjoyed *Quick and the Dead*, I'd be so grateful if you would please review it. Book reviews can make a huge difference to the success of a novel, particularly those of self-published authors like me. If you have time to leave a review, even if it's just a sentence or two, then I'd really appreciate it.

***

Explore the rest of the Silverse…

This book is just one small part of the Silverse, a whole world of vampires that's waiting for you to explore. There are more novels, short stories, serialised story episodes, and even audio drama podcasts. They're all interrelated, although each series stands alone.

Find out more on my website at www.josiejaffrey.com

Acknowledgements

The QuickSilver series has been a decade in the making. It pulls together threads of story littered over hundreds of years' of world-building, and spread across three other separate novel series and a stack of short stories. Finding those threads and lining them up properly to write this central puzzle piece of the Silverse apocalypse has been an absolute undertaking, and one I would never have been able to manage without the unfailing support of my editor Adie Hart. She goes above and beyond to make sure that I haven't borked the continuity or introduced inconsistencies that will tie me in knots later, and she does so with the kind of enthusiasm that keeps me writing when nothing else would. Thank you so much, A, for everything you do.

Huge thanks also to Jen Sugden, my personal cheerleader and bookseller, and wonderful fellow author. I would not have been able to become an audio fiction writer without your support, and I can't wait to explore the podcast world further with you. Big love.

Thanks also to my author buddies Ali Clack and the UKYA Authors Instagram group for their company and support, and to Rachel Bowdler and the Swords & Sapphics Discord for writing with me. Without the sprints channel in that Discord group, I seriously doubt that this series would have been completed so quickly, and I certainly wouldn't have had as much fun doing it.

And thanks to my street team the Silverse Squad, for their unfailing support in promoting my books. I am so grateful.

Finally – and always – thank you to my husband and son, for everything.

CONTENT WARNINGS

General warning for violence/murder.

General warning for extremely graphic blood/gore, including consensual and non-consensual blood drinking, description of injuries, dead bodies, undead body horror, forensic investigation.

Sexual content (mostly consensual, some dubiously consensual due to coercive control).

Some swearing (up to and including 'fuck').

Cult-like community with coercive control.

Emotionally abusive/coercive relationships, including family.

Self-inflicted knife injuries (but not mental health-related self-harm).

Memories of child neglect and abuse.

Uncomfortably sexual behaviour with a quasi-father figure.

Descriptions of being burned.

Discussion of immortal characters buried alive.

Discussion of historical piratical crimes.

Mentions of slavery, both in real/historical context and fantastical/modern context, including keeping humans imprisoned for use as a blood bank.

Mentions of cannibalism.

Zombie apocalypse.